Isle of Dragons

By L. A. Thompson

Prologue

A giant metal centipede marched across the bleak winter landscape, the pilot edging it through the forest. Its multitude of legs crunched against the thick sheet of snow in awkward, sporadic movements. The soft echo of clanking and whirring gears began to slow. The machine flickered in and out of sight, the invisibility setting becoming an increasingly unreliable feature. It soon came to a stop, doing a final sweep of its tail to erase its tracks. After a pause, its hulking body collapsed into the snow, fully visible.

The centipede's mouth lurched open with a loud clunk, and a slight sixteen-year-old scurried from the machine and sprinted to its side. Jade gathered her brown-black hair into a high ponytail before reaching into her cloak. She withdrew an oil can from her robes, murmuring curses while filling the metal beast's crevices with black liquid. Her short tunic and slacks were elegantly stitched but still practical for maneuvering the bulky machine. She surveyed the landscape with a practiced wariness.

Jade tensed. A loud whistling shot through the frigid air. Behind her, a long stream of smoke flowed from a gigantic tank. It bounded toward the edge of the forest, leveling everything in its path. Jade rushed back inside the centipede's mouth, sat in the cockpit, and flicked several switches. The machine responded with a series of mechanical groans, still in plain view and refusing to move.

Toolbox in hand, she hurried back out to the machine's side and flipped open a panel, waving off the steam emitting from the circuitry. Jade jerked her head in the direction of the rapidly encroaching tank. Steadying her breathing, she set down the toolbox, crossed her arms, and held her palms upward, as if drawing energy into them. She closed her eyes and clapped her hands onto the machine. She opened her eyes. Nothing. Her hands fell to her side and she took a deep breath, closing out the sounds around her. She crossed her arms and once again clapped her hands onto the cold metal. A pale blue light ignited around her hands and flowed into the mechanisms. With a click and a whir, the machine roared back to life and became invisible once more.

Jade smiled with relief and triumph. She closed the box and clambered back inside the metal beast's mouth, throwing the toolbox beside her before snapping its mouth shut with the flick of a switch. The centipede crept away from the forest floor and into the underbrush as the tank intruded on her location.

It ground to a halt and the hatch cracked open. A dozen soldiers in white uniforms pounced from the machine, their heavy boots crunching against the snow.

A freckled woman of imposing height strode to the front, the gold insignia of a captain pinned to her cloak. Although Kaylen was only a few years older than Jade, she carried herself with an authority well beyond her years. She sniffed the chilled air irritably, surveying the landscape with a stern and piercing gaze.

"Page," the woman barked. A teenage boy scurried to her side. "Are you sure you sighted her?"

"The reports said that a centipede patrol pod was spotted around these parts," he said.

"All right, spread out and scour the forest," Kaylen ordered. "We need to get her back to the capital as soon as we can." The party split into groups and began their search.

Kaylen marched by the centipede's round, eye-shaped windows. Jade shifted backward, the click of metal centipede legs whirring softly.

"Come out, Jade. There's nothing you can do for your father now. Come home and all will be forgiven."

Jade rolled her eyes. She drew her pod back farther, but a furious tapping on the metal walls made her pause. A small yet strong creature crawled atop the machine. After a couple of rapid scratches, a panel flew off, causing the search party to turn their attention in Jade's direction. A yellow dragon jumped from the machine and slithered out into the open. They jumped back in amazement. It was only slightly bigger than a rat with long, reedy wings folded on its back. The creature hissed at the gathering, slinging its whip-like tail in their direction.

One teenage boy choked back a laugh. "*That's* a dragon?"

The rest of the party laughed, too. “This thing’s nothing like the one back in the capital.”

“That’s enough. Let me handle it,” said Kaylen. The woman removed her spear from her side satchel and flicked on a switch, making the tip sizzle with electricity. The dragon’s eyes widened in fear and alarm before spitting a tiny ball of flame onto her glove, causing it to ignite. She clapped her glove against her side to put it out.

The creature paused, turning its attention away from the gathering. A blue light shined through the trees as someone emerged from deep within the forest. A small and stout-figured young woman, around Jade’s age, held a pan flute to her lips, but there was no sound. The round gemstone that hung around her neck swung side to side in a gentle rhythm with every step she took, giving off a soft glow that radiated throughout the forest.

The dragon stood still, entranced. The young woman waved her hand toward the forest, and the dragon promptly skittered back into the underbrush. She turned to the awestruck crowd while wearing a look of detached amusement.

"How did you do that? What is that?" asked the page.

"No need to thank me. ." Her voice was as sharp as splintered wood. "This is a special flute that only dragons can hear. Tegu dragons are skittish but volatile things. You need to be cautious around them."

The gathering continued to stare.

"Well, I was just passing through. I really must be going." She gave a casual wave and turned to leave.

"You're a witch?" said Kaylen, her grip tightening on the crackling spear.

"Hardly," the woman scoffed, turning back to them with a sigh. "Just a simple trick I picked up." She slid the flute inside her robes.

Whispers of magic weaved through the party as they continued to eye her with suspicion.

"*This* is magic." She crossed her arms and closed her palms, then opened them to reveal a lump of blue powder. She threw it to the ground, creating a puff of smoke that engulfed her. The group's coughs and sputters were followed by mocking, disembodied laughter.

"You shouldn't have wasted your time on me. It seems your target has escaped." When the smoke cleared, the young woman had vanished.

***

She materialized deep in the forest and sauntered off toward a small valley, wearing her self-satisfaction like an old, well-loved coat.

She paused. The hum of an engine approached. A metal centipede appeared before her, grinding to a halt. The mouth cracked open, and Jade soon scurried out. Snow clung to the hollow trees that surrounded them.

"What you did back there was incredible! My name is Jade of House Sol. Thank you for that distraction." She gave a quick bow of gratitude.

"How did you find me?" said Miria.

"I just followed the sparks of magic you left behind. It's a pleasure to meet you, um?"

"I'm just Miria. Miria Atkins. And no need to thank me, I was just passing through. You're not afraid of magic?"

"It can be useful."

Miria turned her attention to the mechanical centipede. "An impressive machine. My brother would love it."

Jade ran a hand along the rusting surface. "Not always reliable, but it's the best I have right now."

"Could I ask why you're so popular, Jade of House Sol?"

"That's complicated," said Jade, averting her gaze. The hiss of the centipede filled the silence. She took in a breath and turned to the other young woman. "You know a few things about dragons. Would you know anything about their home? Or how to get there?"

"You ask a lot of questions. That's not safe, my friend."

"I learned that the hard way," said Jade, her voice cracked and bitter.

Miria gazed up at the snowfall. "The Isle of Dragons is a fairy tale. A bedtime story for children."

"That's clearly not what the nobles think," Jade countered with a slight note of bitterness.

"Well, you know nobility," Miria chuckled. "I'm sorry, Jade of House Sol, but I should be getting home to the farm. I only came because my grandmother sensed trouble. She's good at that, you know. I suggest you find shelter, too. Good luck on your travels." Miria shuffled down the hillside, pulling her cloak tightly about her.

"Wait! Please! I need your help! My father's missing. I heard he was taken to the Isle of Dragons. Can't you tell me anything about how to get there?"

Miria stopped. "I'm sorry, I really am." She continued down the hill.

Jade shuffled through the snow. She couldn't let her only lead slip away.

"Wait," she whispered, her voice rough and desperate. "One night!" she called out. She rifled through the inside of her cloak, withdrawing a fat satchel filled with coins and gave it a light jingle. "I have more if you want it. Just let me stay for one night. I promise that I'll leave in the morning, and you'll never see me again."

Miria turned on her heel, regarding the stranger with an arched brow. Jade opened the satchel and presented the glowing gold coins to the young woman. Her eyes grew large as she tentatively dipped a hand inside to inspect the dozens of glistening coins.

"Well then, what choice do I have?" Miria said as she took the offered satchel and secured it to her belt in a tight knot.

"I suppose we should get out of this snow," Jade suggested.

Miria nodded. "Not the ideal weather for this talk."

Jade dashed inside the centipede's gaping mouth. She motioned to the compartment behind her.

"I should warn you that I've never been good with pods." Once Miria slid into place, she held Jade's shoulder with a viselike grip. It tightened as Jade flicked on switches and the pod began shuffling through the thick layers of snow, making its way down the steep hillside.

"Is it usual for dragons to attack at random?" asked Jade, trying to distract Miria from her uneasiness.

Miria wiped at the foggy porthole on the centipede's left side. "No, not at all. They're rather antisocial things."

"*Life of Dragons* wasn't nonsense after all then," Jade muttered with a note of triumph.

"That old thing? You must be resourceful to have found a copy. The authors wouldn't even write under their real names."

"So, you've read it? They said the Isle of Dragons was a real place, and they were experts in their field."

"They theorized about the possibility, yes. But that was all."

Jade sighed. "Well, do you have any idea what's causing these dragon attacks, like the one in the capital several months back?"

"Were you there for that?"

"It happened in my father's fiefdom. It was a screeching pale creature that died shortly after wreaking havoc. Took everything we had to rebuild."

"That doesn't sound like any dragon I've heard of before. My best guess is that they've gone wild with some kind of infection."

The pod shuffled through the modestly housed village. The rare person who ventured outside stopped to gaze in wonder as they passed. Barren fields and cottages lined their path, the long winter taking its toll on the locals' crops.

When they reached a clearing, Miria tapped Jade's shoulder.

"My home's just a little farther." She pointed to a modest cobblestone cottage with a long trail of smoke flowing from the chimney.

Jade slowed the mechanical centipede until it ground to a halt in front of a dusty wooden barn. She removed her belongings from the pod's mouth and took in her surroundings.

"Welcome to our humble farm," Miria said with a grand, sweeping gesture.

"You're too generous." After weeks on the run, Jade tried to shake off the weariness that fell upon her shoulders like a heavy blanket.

"You won't think that once you meet my family." Miria pointed in the direction of an old tattered woodshed. Baritone murmurs of excitement accompanied the turning of bolts and clanks of metal. The floorboards creaked as Jade followed Miria into the work shed where they were greeted by a stout mechanical bull. A broad-shouldered teenage boy sat on top of it, screwing parts into place with a wrench.

"We won't need that old thing for another season, Dan," Miria's voice rang through the shed. He fell from the mechanical beast with a start.

"You always have to interrupt me while I'm in the middle of caring for Jen." Miria helped him to his feet with a chuckle. "At least you made it back okay. I was starting to worry," he said.

"I can take care of myself, little brother." Miria reached up to ruffle the dust from his brown hair. Jade covered her mouth with her hand to stifle a laugh.

After dusting off his overalls, Dan's fixed his eyes on Jade's pod. He reeled toward it, inspecting every piece in quiet awe.

"You're incredible," he said.

"Maybe you should speak to the owner as well, Dan," said Miria, pointing to Jade.

He picked up his cap from the floor and began shuffling it about in his calloused hands.

"I'm sorry, miss. Just never seen a machine like that before. Good to meet you," said Dan, holding out a hand.

"This is Jade. Of House Sol. I found her in the woods with some less-than-competent pursuers," Miria explained as Jade accepted his firm handshake.

"I was almost expecting you to bring another dragon home as a pet," Dan teased.

"Please, the last time I did that I was ten. And, speaking of juveniles, we'd best go inside. The kids are probably at it again." She turned to the cottage as the yelling grew louder.

"Jade here is a noble with an interest in witchcraft," said Miria. "Maybe you could show us what you can do."

"You're a witch?" Dan asked.

"Of course not," said Jade. "But magic can be a useful tool when you're on the run."

"I always think the best tools are the ones you find in the shed," said Dan with a small shrug.

After setting the mechanical centipede back to invisible, Jade followed the siblings to the cottage.

"It was nice to get away from wild siblings, even for a short time," Dan mused with a note of weariness.

Jade smiled. "I always wanted a brother or sister. I'm sure you're exaggerati—"

The trio was greeted by the sight of a boy of about twelve floating in midair. He floated atop a ball of blue light, clinging to a jar of cookies while an older girl watched on. She tapped her foot impatiently, hands on her hips.

"Gran and Pa made those for a special occasion. Now get down here before you ruin your dinner."

"They didn't say when that occasion was. Why can't we just enjoy them now?"

An elderly man sat by the fireside, engrossed in a book, seemingly unaware of the commotion. He traced each word with a bony finger as he peered over his spectacles, his dark eyes twinkling.

Miria stepped between the boy and girl. "Listen to your sister for once, Avi." She closed her eyes and pinched the bridge of her nose.

The boy descended to the floor and rushed to his sister. "Did you find anything interesting in the forest?" he asked.

"I did, actually." She gestured to Jade, who gave a self-conscious wave.

The two younger siblings turned to the newcomer. "You look like you haven't slept much in a long time," Avi observed.

"I haven't," Jade admitted.

While the boy welcomed her, Elisa locked a questioning stare on her sister. Miria shrugged, turning her attention to the man sitting by the fire.

"Pa, where did Gran get to?" she asked.

"Oh, you're back!" The man put his book on the mantelpiece and hobbled forward to embrace his granddaughter. "Are you all right? Did your grandmother's hunch turn out to be true?"

A husked voice rang from the top of the stairs. "My hunches are always right, Tarin. You should know that by now." A maple wood walking stick clacked against the stairs as a hunched old woman with a crooked smile approached Jade. "Bringing home guests, Miria? The last one you brought home breathed fire and tried to eat the furniture."

"I assure you, I won't do either of those things," said Jade.

"That's good to know at least, right, Gila?" Tarin said with a light chuckle. "But where is our new guest from and what brings you to our old farm?"

"My name's Jade of House Sol, and I was once nobility," she said. "My only family was stolen away to the Isle of Dragons a little while ago. I need your help to find it."

Silence descended.

"Well, I admit that I didn't see this happening," said Gila. "This sounds like a long story."

"You could say that," said Jade, rubbing her aching joints.

"Then please, take a seat." The old woman gestured to the rocking chair. "The best place by the fire is always reserved for the storyteller."

Chapter 1

Rioda Castle was built with a single purpose: to ensure all who entered understood that Vansh was a country built on strength and wealth. The previous king ordered the castle to be remade in the wake of an age of famine and plague, reflecting the rise of a new era.

Its thin spires and high turrets were a warning to anyone who might challenge the kingdom of Vansh. The metal drawbridge snapped out like a serpent's tongue to welcome guests inside, the gates unfurling with a slow clank. A shiver shot down Jade's spine no matter how many times she stepped into the hollow metallic hall.

The men wore heavy woolen tunics and long cloaks while the women wore long dresses that came to their ankles. Jade's clothing always matched those of the other noblewomen. They lifted the sides of their heavy gowns while sliding along the aisle to find a seat close to the proceedings. Everyone chatted amiably and took their seats as if preparing to watch a traveling show that had come to town. Jade exchanged political smiles as she made her way down the row of courtiers and took a seat on the outer rim of the third row. It seemed more like a celebration than a court hearing.

Jade's father, Carison Sol stood before Duchess Ida Roland, whose eyes were unrelenting in their judgment. "You realize that the unnecessary use of your resources is considered treason, Baron Sol?" asked Roland. The Duchess's voice pierced through the great hall like an arrow shot with perfect precision.

"Unnecessary? That dragon left my fiefdom in ruin. We rebuilt homes and the lives of survivors," he replied, deceptively calm.

"You could still have rebuilt with fewer resources. And dragons have a history of random attacks. This is nothing out of the ordinary. We all know what this is," she said.

"I'm sorry, Duchess," he said, looking about in mock bewilderment, "but I don't see the grand scheme that you do."

Roland leaned forward and spoke softly. "You were given a direct order to send men to the front lines. Do you think you have no obligation to our king? Are you questioning and the prophets themselves?"

"I support our king and believe in the prophets. But frankly, I can't see how spending years abroad on a crusade to battle dragons is fulfilling that prophecy to bring us to a new, brighter era."

Indignant cries echoed throughout the grand hall. Jade put a hand to her mouth in shock and amusement.

Roland stood and cleared her throat. When the crowd eventually quieted, she resumed her seat. "As much as you seem to resent that I am upholding the orders and traditions of our royalty, I still uphold them. Dragon attacks are nothing new, and we did what we could to cull them in the old days, and we'll continue to do so. Now, as for your sentence—"

"That's not true!" said Jade, rising from her seat.

"What isn't true, dear?" Roland drummed her finger on the arm of her chair, eyes boring into Jade's.

She shook off the urge to shrink down under that gaze. "Dragons don't have a history of attacks. They're known for keeping to themselves. This has only happened fairly recently. The old writings on dragons—"

"Are myths, my dear. It's our duty to focus on our current issues, which is helping Marda and expanding our great empire," said Roland.

Jade winced at the mention of her mother's home.

"The country would be in ruins if not for the efforts of King Jarrod," Roland added.

"I'd say it's already in ruins. My fiefdom certainly was after a dragon attacked, seemingly out of nowhere. Quite strange, don't you think?" Carison asked with mock innocence.

The renewed shouts of outrage roared in Jade's ears like rushing water.

Roland's command for silence pierced the outraged voices in the hall, which gradually faded to bitter mutterings before dying out altogether.

"I have lost my patience with you, Sol. Despite our attempts to be reasonable, you continue to defy king and country. I hereby strip you of your rank and sentence you to the gallows."

Jade stood, took a deep breath, and put everything she'd learned in court as a diplomat to use. "My lords and ladies, I don't believe expelling someone whose house has served the royal family for generations is sending a good message during these times. This nation—"

"Is in danger when the servants of the crown act in an insubordinate manner. I'm afraid we can't afford to show any more leniency than we already have."

Jade slumped in her seat, avoiding the hard gazes of the other nobles.

"All of your worldly possessions shall be wiped from your name." Roland waved to the guards.

Jeers filled the room as Carison was led from the hall.

Jade followed, ignoring the crowd. "Grant!"

A gangly young man with close-cropped brown hair shot a sympathetic look at Jade. He stopped and waited.

"Could we have a moment?" Jade asked.

The guard nodded with a respectful bow, taking a step back.

Jade took a deep breath. She and Carison looked at one another for another moment, unsure of what to say.

"I only made things worse for you," she muttered.

Carison held up a pale hand. "You know they've been after me for a long time now. I'm only surprised they hadn't found a way to do this sooner," he admitted with a weary smile.

Jade wanted to disagree, convinced there must have been something she could have done.

He turned to the guard. "Can she stay with your family, Grant? Your old man said he'd help if it came to this."

He gave a firm nod. "Of course."

"Well then, we'd better be going." Carison looked to Jade one last time. He slipped a hand inside his pocket, withdrawing a small gold key and pressing it into her hands. "In case you should need it," he whispered. She wrapped her fist around it. "Be well, Jade. And try to find happiness. It's what your mother would have wanted." His footsteps echoed through the long, empty hall as Jade watched her father's back fade from her sight. She slid the key into her robes and left the castle alone.

***

Jade spent her days after the trial sewing and helping Grant's mother around the Edist family estate. They weren't nobility, but the Edists had a history of guardsmen and soldiers loyal to the crown, so they lived in good standing. Grant kept Jade updated on Carison's condition when he came home each night.

The weeks passed in relative quiet until one afternoon when Grant's mother was taking Jade through sewing a quilt. Suddenly, Grant arrived home from the castle in a disheveled state, rushing into the sewing room to find them. Panting and wild-eyed he cried," Jade! It's your father!"

"Grant, please, don't come barging into here like that. What are you even doing here at this hour?" said his mother.

"I…I'm sorry!" he stammered with a quick bow. "But I need to speak with Jade now."

"Couldn't this wait until later?" Grant's mother shot him a disapproving look.

"Jade needs to hear this now." He beckoned her to leave the sewing room with a flick of his hand.

"Excuse me, ma'am." Jade bowed before leaving the room.

Grant held Jade by the shoulders when she joined him in the hallway. "His cell! It's empty!" Grant's tone held a note of panic.

"W…what are you talking about?" Jade took a step away from the young guard.

"I overheard Kaylen talking outside the prison. She said they're taking him and a group of others to the Isle of Dragons."

"You can't be serious?" Jade scoffed.

"She said there was a ship leaving tonight."

Jade opened the shutters of a nearby window, gazing out at the Vanshian sea. "Then I'll have to see for myself."

"I suppose I could try talking to Kaylen," said Grant.

"She doesn't listen to us anymore, only her 'superiors' in the guard and the court," Jade mumbled, her gaze traveling outside the stained glass window and to the field they roamed in their childhood.

"They won't like you snooping around," Grant warned.

"It'll be fine," she huffed, refusing to look away from the sea. "Somehow."

Late that night, Jade crept onto the docks, Grant trailing behind her. They peered from behind a decrepit old boat shed. Men and women tied in a long line ascended the ramp of a large metal ship.

"I told you!" Grant whispered.

Jade ran behind a crate, inching closing to the ship for a better look.

"Come back!" Grant hissed.

She turned to him, mouthing the words, "Go back."

He took in a breath, hesitating a moment before running home.

Jade inspected the new group trudging up the ramp. Her father was at the start of the line. They locked eyes. His mouth fell open, and he tried to yell out to her, but a guard pushed him onto the ship from behind.

A soldier suddenly grabbed her from behind, putting a hand around her shoulders. "Damn Sols can't stay out of trouble!" Riley cackled as he dragged her away.

Kaylen sauntered onto the dock, staring down at with a stern glare. Jade held her head high, meeting her gaze with defiance. Her fists shook with fear.

Kaylen sighed. "Just this once, I'll let you go with a warning."

"What happened to you, Kay? You looked up to Father, and he did so much for you."

"There's nothing to admire about a traitor," Kaylen murmured. She took in a breath and lowered herself to meet Jade's gaze. "You won't tell anyone what you saw here tonight. Understood? No one will believe a disgraced noble's daughter, anyway. Forget what you saw, and try to start over. Now leave."

"Wait," Jade cried. As Kaylen turned to leave, Jade crossed her arms at the wrist and created a thin blue rope of light that wrapped loosely around the woman's wrist.

Kaylen glared down in fear at the blue light, and she jumped back, the light quickly fading into nothingness. “What was that?” she demanded. Riley backed away from Jade

“I-I don’t know!” Jade’s voice trembled. “I’m sorry! That just happened somehow.”

‘Take her back to the Edist estate!’ Kaylen growled, backing away from Jade.

“But…” Riley protested.

“I said take her back!”

Riley and the guards escorted Jade back to the Edist estate in silence. “Better watch this one,” muttered Riley. “She’s dangerous.”

“What are you talking about?” asked Grant’s mother.

“I’ll explain!” Jade snapped, her gaze wild and panicked.

“You do that,” said Grant’s father, gesturing for the guards to leave with a wave if his hand.

Riley shot Jade a glare before leaving with the guards, closing the door behind them.

“I am so sorry for sneaking out and causing you trouble, but I saw my father at the docks! They’re taking him to the Isle!”

"I'm sure you only imagined seeing him," said Grant's mother, her tone calm and placating. She exchanged a swift, nervous glance with her husband. "I understand how hard all this must be, but you can't believe what you're saying."

Jade stuttered, struggling to form words. She looked to Grant, who stared down at the floor, shuffling his feet.

"It's been a long night. Why don't we all get some rest?" Grant's father suggested.

Later in the night, Jade wandered the halls. She couldn't sleep. The events on the dock running through her mind repeatedly.

As Jade passed the dining room, Grant's parents sat around the table, cloaks draped around their shoulders as they drank from large mugs.

"I like the girl, I do," whispered Grant's mother. "But we can't keep her here. Now that she doesn't even have a title to her name, marriage is out of the question."

Jade dug her fingers into the side of her nightdress. She was right. No one would want to marry the daughter of a disgraced ex-noble. There was no future for her in Rioda.

"I took her in as a favor to an old friend," said Grant's father, rubbing his temples. "Let's just leave things for now. There aren't many places she can go, after all."

Jade slinked back to her room. In the following days, she spent her nights staring up at the ceiling, replaying that night on the docks. She came up with a plan.

One evening, Jade hastily packed everything she owned into a knapsack. Grant leaned against the doorway. "So, you're leaving?"

She turned to him and gazed out into the hallway. The people gathered in the portrait hanging on the wall seemed to regard her with a distant unease.

"There isn't a place for me here," she said, brushing past him.

"Where will you go?"

Jade paused. "I need to pay one last visit to the Sol estate before searching for answers."

"You're going to need a lot of luck," said Grant.

"Thank you for everything." Jade looked over her shoulder with a tired smile before walking away.

"You have nothing to thank me for," Grant muttered to the empty room.

***

A full moon lit the sky when Jade crept into the Sol estate's armory. Another noble family was soon to move in, so it was only occupied by guards. A fire burned at the estate entrance with soldiers laughing and drinking around the flames to a tune played on a lyre. Some had served her father before she was even born. Although, their numbers were low since most were sent to the front, as per Duchess Roland's wishes. Jade held onto the hope that she could convince the soldiers to pretend they hadn't seen her if they caught her. However, most were too drunk and tired to notice anything.

She inched closer, ducking and weaving behind barrels and crates. Books and tunics and dresses that belonged to Jade and her family smoldered in the fire. She dug her fingernails into the crate she hid behind, resisting the urge to take hold of a nearby tarp and throw it on the fire. Jade rushed out from behind the crate and dashed inside the armory. The Sol family's estate housed a larger armory than most noble families. It stretched far and was lined with a row of centipede pods, at the ready to patrol the fiefdom.

Jade slinked through the room until she reached a large ceremonial suit of armor with the Sol family crest emblazoned on the front. The suit gently clattered as Jade pushed the armor to one side. Panting with the effort, she finally moved it far enough to reveal a doorway. She shuffled inside her robes, removing a key. She inserted it into the lock, twisting it until a soft click signaled for her to push the creaking door open. Jade peered over her shoulder before stepping inside, checking for a guard who may have followed her. When a long silence replied to her fears, she shuffled into a dank narrow passage, pressing the door behind her closed.

Down the narrow hall lay a treasure chest which Jade silently approached. She cranked the key into the lock and pushed the chest open, revealing pieces of gold and silver filling it to the brim, along with several bulky satchels filled with coins. Jade packed as many as she could fit inside the knapsack while tucking others into the insides of her robes.

Mingled voices echoed through the hall, their laughter distant yet strangely familiar. Jade packed her coins away into her robes and trailed the faint sounds along the passageway. She kept an ear close to the wall; the voices growing louder when she reached the library. Laughter filled the room. She peered inside the eyeholes of a portrait. An old man in a thick white cloak spoke to someone out of Jade's line of sight.

"Well, I'll be leaving now. Do enjoy your new home," he said.

"I will. You must thank your mistress the Duchess for arranging this," Kaylen Jacobs stepped forward, shaking the man's hand.

Jade clapped a hand over her mouth to hold back a gasp.

Kaylen's gaze shot to the portrait.

"Did you hear something?" the man asked.

"It's hard to say," Kaylen said, cocking an eyebrow.

Jade moved away, pressing her back against the wall.

"Guards!" Kaylen ran onto the porch. "Search every corner of the castle! It seems we have an intruder. I want you to find them and bring them to me!"

"Yes, ma'am!" the men-at-arms chorused.

"Act swiftly; I suspect this is more than just a common thief. The capital's safety may depend on finding them. Now go."

The guards dispersed throughout the estate. Kaylen retreated back inside and returned with a spear, joining the search.

Jade bolted down the passage, depositing some coins along the way to lighten her load. She closed the trapdoor, thrusting the picture back in place before shuffling into the mouth of the nearest centipede pod, her footsteps echoing against the metal as she slipped behind the control panel Four soldiers filed into the armory as its mouth snapped shut.

"Search every patrol pod," Riley barked. The guards began inspecting the inside of each metal beast. Jade's fingers lingered over the control board. She muttered the sequence to turn on the metal centipede, taking deep, slow breaths as the guards approached her pod.

"You won't find your thief here," a hoarse voice muttered from the entrance. Grant leaned against the doorway, panting frantically.

Jade resisted the urge to open the hatch and shout for him to leave.

"What are you doing here, royal guard?" Riley spat.

"During my patrol of the tower, I saw an intruder sneaking into the estate from the parapets." Grant stiffened, regaining his composure. "They entered through the guards' quarters. So, unless you want to spend the next few weeks without booze money, I suggest you get over there."

While a few of the soldiers filed out of the armory and left to inspect the guards' quarters, several remained behind.

Riley remained fixed in place, glaring at Grant with folded arms. "Who gave you permission to leave your post in the middle of the night?"

Grant shrugged, shifting his feet slightly as he cleared his throat. "Does it matter? Is it so hard to believe that the royal guards want to help a fellow guard during these uncertain times?"

Riley lunged at Grant, waves of electricity flying from his spear. Grant took a step back, parrying the blow using a spear with a tip that crackled with electricity.

"You'll never work as a guard again if the new master finds out that you attacked a high-ranking soldier's son," a man cautioned.

Riley continued to strike blow after blow while the other young man struggled to evade them. "Your family's housing the traitor's daughter, aren't they? Why are you really here, royal guard?" He snarled Grant's title as if he were making a threat, grappling the spear from his hands, and shoving him to the ground. He held the spear to Grant's chest.

The hatch of Jade's pod snapped open. "Grant, stop!"

Everyone stopped and turned to Jade.

The guards looked to one another. "The baron's daughter," they whispered.

"Guards, please, honor the time you spent in my father's service and pretend you never saw me here."

Riley stalked toward her, spear ignited, and eyes blazing with a single-minded focus. 'Why would I honor a traitor and a witch?'

"I'm not a witch," Jade said, a tremor in her voice.

"Just let her go, boy. She's already lost everything," said a senior guard.

He ignored the man, continuing forward.

Grant scrambled to his feet and ran toward another guard, wrestling the spear from his grasp. "Jade, go!"

Jade froze. "Not without you!"

"Go!" said Grant with a wry smile. "I'll be fine. Somehow. Be free of this place."

Jade retreated into the pod and flashed the lights on. Its multitude of legs began peddling along the walls of the armory. She glanced over her shoulder one last time. Riley bolted to the pods, but Grant blocked his way, jamming his spear against the other guards. She flicked on the stealth setting and the invisible creature skittered toward the estate's entrance. The beeps and hums of Vanshian code blared over the radio, automatically transmitting to each pod and tracking her movements. Jade jumped and yanked at the radio system's wires until they came loose, and the sound died out.

Kaylen halted during her patrol of the estate's tower, catching a glimpse of snow falling atop the invisible centipede's body. "She's getting away! The girl's getting away in a patrol pod!"

Kaylen propelled her spear toward the mechanical creature, and the electric tip hit a back panel, jolting the centipede back into sight. Jade gripped the controls tighter and cursed under her breath, flipping the stealth setting switch back and forth, as the machine erratically flickered in and out of visibility. She pulled the control lever toward her, forcing the mechanical creature to move with as much speed as it could muster. The centipede skittered away from the estate and into the thick underbrush, disappearing into the night.

Chapter 2

Jade lay back in the rocking chair, closing her eyes. “I left them behind. Both Grant and my father.”

“You didn’t have any other choice,” said Tarin.

“So, you’ve made it all this time on your own?” Gila asked.

“I used what I could to get by,” said Jade, patting the knapsack full of coins beside her. “Now, I just need to figure out a way to get to the Isle,” Jade said with a sardonic laugh, pressing a hand to her forehead.

Avi sat cross-legged on the woolen carpet, swaying in quiet confusion. Elisa shifted about on the floor next to him, tracing the patterns on the carpet.

Miria gazed into the burning embers of the fire. “Well, that explains all the fuss over one missing noble,” she muttered.

Dan gazed at his grandparents, watching their reaction, his expression unreadable.

Gila and Tarin shared a tired glance, “So, you won’t stop until you find that forsaken place?” muttered Gila.

Jade snapped into a standing position and bowed her head in a swift motion. "We have a bargain that I will only stay for the night in exchange for money and answers about the Isle.

"Good," Elisa muttered under her breath, low enough so that her grandparents would not hear.

"No need for formalities here, girl." Gila motioned for Jade to sit, but she remained standing, hands by her side in a stiff posture. "But your pod needs repairs, and Dan might be good, but it will probably take him longer than a night to finish the job."

Jade took a breath and rubbed at her shoulder. For the first time, she noted the aches and pains she had gathered during the weeks spent inside a cramped pod.

"Now, please sit. I have something to ask you," Gila commanded. Jade resumed her seat.

"Gila, don't," Tarin protested. She held up a hand in response.

"Please, Tarin, this is important." She turned her attention back to Jade. "It is unfortunate about your father. But supposing you did find him; what will you do? Will you live on the Isle, on the run from those who sent him there in the first place? If you make it home, you'll still live on the run."

"You don't know that," Jade whispered.

“We can help,” Dan interrupted. “Miria here knows more about Mom and Dad’s work than anyone.”

“What are you talking about?” asked Jade.

Miria sighed. “You know, Jade of House Sol, maybe Gran isn’t wrong. It might be better if you find somewhere to lie low and—”

“Hope that one day he’ll return?” said Jade. “Live alone with no person or place I can call home? Please, I’m only asking you to point me in the right direction.”

“Any who’ve tried to reach the Isle have failed,” said Tarin. “I’m sorry, but there’s nothing more you can do.”

Jade shook her head. “You wouldn’t understand.”

Elisa shot Jade a piercing glare.

“You remind me far too much of someone I knew. Why don’t you put away your things, and we’ll continue this talk later, all right?” Gila suggested with a weary sigh. “Elisa, show Jade to her room.”

The younger girl huffed in protest but still led Jade up the stairs, motioning for her to follow with a flick of the hand.

Jade gathered her belongings and nodded in thanks. She made her way up the stairs, averting her eyes all the while. Elisa guided her to a room at the end of the hall. She regarded the older girl with a stern glare, and she turned to leave.

"We don't need this kind of trouble," she murmured. "Oh…and there's a bath at the end of the hall to your right." Elisa pointedly gestured at Jade's clothes before stomping down the stairs.

Jade clung to her sweat-soaked tunic. The last few weeks allowed her little time to rest or change. "Oh, t…thanks," she replied with a nervous laugh.

After bathing in the family's cramped wooden tub and putting on a change of clothes, she began packing her things away in the drawers. They were empty except for a frayed piece of paper with handwriting. Burning with curiosity, Jade unfolded it, pushing any feelings of guilt aside. Large, elegant handwriting graced a scrap of paper.

The Isle of Dragons is a real place filled with mystery and wonder. We will be the first ones to return from there. We promise. And when we do, we'll show it to you, too. In the meantime, take care of one another.

Goodbye, for now.

Mom & Dad.

P.S. Tell your Gran and Pa to stop worrying.

Jade tucked the letter back where she found it, easing the drawer closed. She allowed exhaustion to wash over her for the first time in too long when a sudden rapping at her door made her jump.

"Time for dinner," Elisa snapped, rolling her eyes.

Jade shuffled behind the girl on their way to the dining room. She was about to speak when Tarin greeted her at the foot of the steps, "Come, Jade. We have something special for you." He waved, escorting her to the dining room. A large feast lined the table with many dishes Jade had never seen before.

"You need some proper food," said Gila, spotting Jade while setting the table.

"Just like back home in Nyonan," chorused the children in unison.

"I wasn't going to say it this time," Gila grumbled with the trace of a smile.

"You really didn't have to go to all this trouble," said Jade.

"Of course, we did," Gila scoffed. "You're our guest. And besides, we harvested enough before winter that we can afford to indulge now and then."

"Miria knew winter was coming early this season. She saw the dragons weren't heading off to hibernate. So, we decided we needed to harvest early, and now we've got plenty," Dan explained.

"Not that many in this town would listen," said Gila. "This damned winter's not natural, and they don't see it. And rumors say other nations are experiencing seemingly never-ending winters. That or droughts." Gila gestured to Miria. "At least you had the good sense to know something was happening."

"I know my parents' work," Miria said, brushing a hand through her long braid. "They understood dragons, and other creatures from the Realm of Magic.You need to see this, Jade of House Sol." She withdrew a notebook from her robes and clapped it open on the table. The page opened on an intricately drawn map of the southern lands. Marda lay at the center. Beyond the massive gulf at the country's southeast was a large circle-shaped island. A question mark above the words "the Isle of Dragons" was scrawled out at the top of the page.

"Our mother drew this during a research expedition with Father before they wrote *Life of Dragons*," Miria explained.

"This is it," Jade breathed. "Mother never told me it was so close to Marda."

"These were drawn from stories told by sailors about their encounters with the waters surrounding the Isle," said Miria. "There are strange stories about those encounters, most thought they were just the ramblings of seafarers with too much time and drink in them."

"They say it's a cursed island and the waters are meant to keep humans out. If your father's there, your friends must have somehow found a way past those barriers."

Jade traced a hand over the drawings and took in a breath. "You don't know how much this means to me." She suddenly drew Miria into a tight embrace.

"Well, Jade of…Jade," said Miria, awkwardly untangling herself from the other girl and clearing her throat. "Now you have more information on the Isle, as promised."

Jade cleared her throat promptly and mumbled an apology, taken aback by the sudden action. "Now I have a route to the Isle," she said. "Now I can make plans."

"Before plans, we need to eat," Gila said while waving her stick in the direction of the food.

Jade and the Atkins family gathered around the table and shared the food in the middle of the table. The pale blue stone around Miria's neck gleamed brightly, and everyone around the table raised a hand to shield their eyes from it.

"What kind of stone is that? It doesn't look like anything from this world," Jade said, shielding her face from its brightness.

A dragon's roar echoed in the distance. "Sorry, it does that when dragons are nearby. It's from the realm of magic. Dragons are creatures of magic, and where the flute gets dragons' attention, this keeps it." Miria tucked the stone under her shawl, only slightly dimming its light. "It was a gift after Father helped an injured deer on the side of the road while studying in Marda. You could say he was a little surprised when the recovered deer thanked him by transforming into a human man."

"A shapeshifter?" Jade chortled in shock and surprise. "They're not just a fairy tale?"

"If only they were," mumbled Gila.

"He couldn't understand my father's horror at a naked man standing in the place of a deer!"

"There's so much we don't know about the other realm," Jade said with a chuckle.

"Most people are too scared to know. So they rejected my parents and their work."

"They needed more recognition," said Jade.

"What they needed was to stay here," said Gila in a low murmur, as if an old, bitter memory were creeping up on her.

"Please, Gila," Tarin said in a low voice. "We agreed; not in front of the children."

"Maybe they thought there was something better than being here," Miria remarked, between bites of her food.

Dan and Elisa kept their gaze firmly on her meal, trying to follow her grandparents' exchange, Avi began to fidget with his food and uncomfortably shifted about in his seat.

Jade's mind wandered to the letter lying at the bottom of the drawer. "I'm sorry," she whispered.

"You're not the one who should be sorry, girl. This family just likes to speak their mind a little too much," Gila waved off her apology. The old woman glanced over at the family, who avoided her gaze.

Silence resumed until they had finished their meal. Gila crossed her arms, closed her eyes, then waved toward the plates. They promptly rose from the table and arranged themselves on the dining room bench in a slow yet orderly fashion.

Jade blinked. "You know magic, too?"

"Who do you think taught Miria and this troublemaking monkey?" said Gila, chuckling at Avi's muttered protests.

'If I could just master magic when I need to, I wouldn't need to stay here.'

'In my experience, you never so much master it as you form a partnership with it,' said Gila. 'Have you ever tried using it?'

'I've done enough magic to get myself out of trouble, like when my pod wouldn't move,' said Jade.

'But it didn't fix your pod, did it?' Gila asked.

'It still needs repairs.'

'Exactly. We're only drawing on the magic in the universe for a flash of assistance. It might take you a short distance if you need to be somewhere in a hurry, or protect you from harm, but magic can't solve everything that comes, as much as we might want it to.'

'I stopped learning for a long time,' Jade admitted.

'I could teach you if you'd like,' Avi offered.

'Thank you, but I'll be leaving in the morning,' she patted the boy's hand.

'About that,' said Tarin. 'Gila and I would like you to stay. You can live here for as long as you like.'

"Thank you, but I'll be leaving in the morning." She patted the boy's hand.

"About that," said Tarin. "Gila and I would like you to stay. You can live here for as long as you like."

"That's very kind of you," Jade said, stiffening slightly and averting her gaze, the memory of the last time someone took her in still fresh in her mind. "But I need to get to my father as soon as I can."

"You said you'd figure out the plan from here, right?" said Miria. "You can stay here while you figure out the details."

"Please stay," said Gila. "We insist."

Jade's shoulders slumped as she forced a smile. "I'll have to move on as soon as my pod's fixed."

"You're welcome here as long as you need," said Tarin. "We couldn't save our daughter and son-in-law, but maybe we can help you in some small way."

"I'll make your pod as good as new," said Dan. Avi nodded along with a large grin, excited to have a guest.

Elisa kept her head down. "Why should we house someone on the run?" she murmured.

"Because we can and we should," Gila said with a note of finality.

"I can pay you again when I leave," Jade promised them, bowing her head.

"For now, you can get some rest." The old woman gestured for the family to head upstairs. "You can stock up on supplies for your journey after you've settled in and the weather has calmed down a little."

Jade nodded. She made her way up to her room and sprawled out onto the bed and fell into a deep sleep. It was her first peaceful night's sleep, free of the cramped space of her pod, for the first time since she left the capital.

Chapter 3

Dan piloted his old creaky metal bull into town. It ground to an abrupt halt once it had reached the marketplace. Jade gripped Dan's waist tightly as the machine jerked back and forth.

"I can see why your sister doesn't like pods much."

"I know she's a rickety old thing, but she'll hold together." Dan flicked a switch that eased the pod down into the snow.

The bull's side hatch fell open with a groan, and they marched down the hatch and into the marketplace. The pair weaved through the small crowd; the shops littered throughout the town were small and shabby with faded paint and weary-faced owners. A barn owl with piercing, pale blue eyes and ruffled feathers perched on a fence, its head swiveling about as it scanned the crowd. Jade gazed up at the owl, who briefly meet her gaze before flying away.

They continued until they approached a stall with a collection of pipes, metal panels and coils, and various other parts lined up neatly.

"You should probably go ahead without me," said Dan. "I'll meet you back at the pod."

An old man eyed them from the stall while polishing a piece of metal.

"I thought you loved anything to do with pods?"?" Jade said as she caught sight of the man approaching out of the corner of her eye, his gaze stern and cold.

"Haven't seen you around here lately," the man said with a snarl.

"I was just moving on, sir." Dan glanced at Jade and tipped his hat. "I'll see you soon."

"Wait!" She placed a hand on his shoulder.

"Saddling up with the nobles, are you?" the man asked as he gestured at Jade's finely embroidered clothing. "Having good connections won't change what you are."

"And what is that, exactly?" said Jade. She arched an eyebrow and stiffened her back in the same manner her mother had taught her when someone in court asked an impertinent question.

"Pardon my bluntness, miss, but that whole family is mad. They're into the strange and unnatural. They've caused crops to die out. They caused this," he said, waving at the snowfall with a wild gesture. "Walk away now before they drag you into their…pit of lunacy."

"I appreciate the advice," she said with a sharpness foreign to her ears. "But I can make my own decisions." Jade politely inclined her head before walking away, leaving the man dumbfounded. "Come on, Dan. We'll just have to find somewhere else to find our supplies."

He glared back, eyebrows raised. "Good luck," the man said, returning to polishing the piece of metal.

"What was that all about?" Jade said as they strode away. Dan guided her out of the line of stalls, and they sat on a creaky old bench before brushing the piling snowflakes from it.

"We're not all that popular with everyone. We can be trouble," said Dan, removing his cap, shuffling it about in his calloused hands.

"I'm the one with the gaggle of guards on my trail while I chase after a place no one's returned from," Jade said with a wry chuckle.

"I always wanted to see it," Dan admitted. "The Isle, I mean. It sounded like the kind of place you could only read about in myths. But I was told again and again that it is real."

"I wanted to see Marda so badly. My mother talked about it so many times, especially right before…" Jade scuffed her feet through the snow. "She was the ambassador to Marda. I can't even remember half of the stories she told about Marda now."

"My parents' stories are pretty hazy for me, too," said Dan. "But Miria keeps their work going as much as she can. You're a lot alike, you know."

"Could we move on, please?" Jade asked.

Dan nodded and promptly led her back to the market, where they moved through the stalls and found the items for the pod and their home. Jade jingling her coins about ensured they returned with more supplies than needed.

***

Jade explained the morning's events to the family over tea while Dan and Elisa put the supplies away in the work shed.

"You stood up to the cranky old goat? Good for you," said Miria. She raised her teacup in a gesture of respect before taking a sip.

"I'm sorry you had to experience the joy of our rural existence like that," Gila added.

Jade shook her head. "I'm sorry that you have so much to deal with."

"We have even more to deal with now," Elisa muttered as she entered the room with Dan. She threw a pointed glare at Jade.

"Can you give it a rest?" Dan removed his filthy boots before slumping into the chair by the fire.

Elisa ignored him, looking to Jade. "This might be a nice guest house for you, but I have work to do. The chicken coop is still a mess," she muttered as she stomped outside with a basket and hammer.

"She's always like that," Avi assured Jade with a shrug.

"It's fine," Jade said with a dismissive wave. "If you'll excuse me, I'll be in my room." She bowed and made her way to the stairs.

"Wait. My room. Now," said Miria just as Jade began to climb the stairs. "We need to do something with those clothes. Should have done this from the start."

Jade paused in realization. "I stand out too much, of course. I've already drawn unwanted attention." She pressed a hand to her forehead and sighed at her own thoughtlessness.

"Let's just find some suitable clothes for you to wear," said Miria. She moved past Jade and led the way to her room. She motioned for Jade to sit on the bed while she rifled through her wardrobe.

"Why are you helping me?"

"You stood up for Dan. That boy's too easygoing for his own good. Besides, someone needs to dress you," said Miria, her smile cracked to the side.

"I don't belong here."

"Then you're part of an exclusive club," said Miria with a shrug. She threw yet another article of clothing on the bed.

Jade raised a finger in protest. However, after trying and failing to resist the urge due to the soreness that still clung to her after weeks in a stuffy pod, she decided not to say anything.

"Besides, it's too late," said Miria. "We've already dragged you into our pit of lunacy." Miria guided Jade behind her tall pinewood dresser, shoving a pile of clothes into her arms before sitting on a stool on the other side of the dresser.

"I could find an inn while I wait for the repairs," said Jade while trying on an old dress. "I already have the information I need."

Tapping on the side of the stool, Miria muttered, "Don't you think you should have someone with you?"

"I'll have to pay a crew to take me to Isle once I get to Marda. It will work if I have enough denarans and I exchange them for cadans."

"It's not wise to travel alone, especially where you're going."

"The fewer people involved in this, the better," murmured Jade.

"I see," Miria said, her shoulders falling. "Well, you'll have to figure out the rest from here."

Jade emerged from the dresser in a simple blue gown and a pair of work boots. "Well," she said, holding up her arms and examining her new garments. "How do I look?"

"Like a farmer," Miria said, clapping a hand on Jade's shoulder. "My work here is done."

Jade gave a swift bow in gratitude, before rising to her feet. "Well. I suppose I have some there," she said, pointing downstairs toward Elisa's general direction.

"You have nothing to do on that front. Don't worry. She'll come around," Miria assured with a shrug.

Jade took a breath and headed to the chicken coop. Elisa ignored her as she hammered a plank of wood into the doorway.

"It should start snowing again," Jade said, looking to the bleak, overcast sky.

"You almost look like you belong here." Elisa glanced at the older girl with a critical eye before continuing with her work.

"I can help," Jade offered.

"I thought this kind of work would be beneath a noble."

Jade crouched beside the younger girl. "I can't call myself one anymore."

"If Dan wasn't always telling her not to make a fuss, Miria would have told off that nasty old fart years ago," Elisa said in a contemplative tone.

Jade's shoulders shook before releasing a hearty chortle that surprised them both. "So, I did something right then?"

"Please pass that." Elisa gestured to a wooden board. Jade promptly complied. "Do you think you can handle farm work, ex-noble?"

"I spent weeks in a cramped pod. I think I can handle some chores," Jade said with an indignant scowl and a slight pout.

"We'll see," Elisa scoffed, her lips twitching upward in what almost seemed like a smile.

Chapter 4

An oily rag slung over his shoulder, a greasy-faced Dan burst into the dining room while Jade and the rest of the Atkins family ate their morning meal.

"Pa, Gran, I'm going to need some help," Dan said in a hoarse voice, wiping grease from his hands with the dirty old rag.

"Are you losing your voice because you sang too much while working on pods again?" Elisa asked with a bored expression.

"No," said Dan. "But someone should equip pods with a way to play music."

"What is the help that you need, boy?" Gila prompted.

"Right," he said, clearing his throat. "Jade, more than one of your pod's legs fell off. This weather makes the trim pieces on a pod far more brittle. We'll have to replace it," he explained with an apologetic smile.

"Oh," said Jade. "I didn't want to impose on you much longer."

"We barely found enough wires and scraps to improvise with the repairs," said Dan.

"Why don't you head to Old Rosh's?" Tarin suggested.

"Old Rosh?" asked Dan. He tossed his oily rag from one hand to another as he contemplated the significance behind the name. "Oh, you mean the Mechanic?" His eyes brightened into a smile. "Do you really think he'd see us?"

"You talk about him like he's a spirit!" Miria said with a teasing cackle.

"Who is this Mechanic? Where can I find him?" asked Jade.

"He's a legendary figure for pod enthusiasts," said Dan. "He collects pod parts from all around and repairs all kinds of pods. He's even been known to make them for farmers who can't afford one. He lives on the edges of Nearwood Forest. Very few know much about him."

“He’s a cranky, disagreeable old fella, but he makes a good lemon pie,” Gila said, leaning back in her chair and looking up at the ceiling with a nostalgic grin.

“All right then,” said Jade, rising from her place at the table and sliding her chair back. “I’ll be going. May I please borrow your pod?”

“Do you know where Nearwood is?” asked Miria.

“I passed it on my way here. I went by an old, rundown hut.”

“Sounds like Rosh’s place,” said Tarin.

“The Mechanic is known for not liking visitors, but if I come with you and explain that I’m the grandson of two of his friends, then I’m sure he’ll be happy to help us,” Dan said, bouncing on the balls of his feet at the prospect of meeting his hero.

“Friend might be too strong a word, but you would be better off taking Dan with you,” Gila said. “He is the one repairing your centipede, after all. Besides, he’ll be able to learn something from the old boy.”

"You probably would know the way better than I would," Jade admitted. "Please lead the way." She turned to Dan with a sweeping bow.

"Please, we've told you there's no need to be so formal."

Jade followed behind Dan to the work shed, the roar of the old mechanical bull signaling the beginning of their trek into Nearwood.

***

The mechanical bull plowed into the forest with all the finesse associated with the beast that inspired it. They sat cramped inside, with Jade seated behind Dan. Its metallic hooves crushed the small bushes and shrubbery beneath it.

"Not the quietest of things, but this old beast is all we've got," Dan mumbled from the pilot seat.

"Wait! What's that?" asked Jade. The sloping hill ahead of them formed a semicircle of brittle trees with tangled branches that twisted and stretched into pincer-like nibs. They surrounded a wide and muddy bog that smelled fouler than any smell that they could recall and bubbled threateningly as the pod slipped lower down the hill and inside of it.

“Dan, hurry! We need to back up!”

“Getting there, getting there.” His voice also rose as the mechanical hooves trotted gingerly backward. The bull made it back up the hill, its movements sluggish and labored. They kept moving until the mechanical beast chugged past a large estate with a discarded and rusting centipede pod resting outside.

“That looks about the same size as your pod!” Dan yelled from over his shoulder.

“It’s much older and rustier than mine. We could probably still salvage it for parts.”

Dan shrugged his shoulders. “On the other hand, whoever owns that estate might know who you are. And if we manage to find the Mechanic, it won’t be necessary. We better go.”

However, before they moved on, the sound of a much larger pod roared toward the estate. Although they could not see anything, the surrounding underbrush was pressed down by the pressure of something large with quietly whirring gears and which hissed as it released a thin stream of smoke from its top. A series of figures cloaked in black robes scurried from the invisible intruder and busily inspected the centipede. They removed gears, pivots, and coils before placing them in the machine's back compartment with care. Once they had finished and the centipede pod had fewer of its distinguishing features, the figures climbed back into the pod, and the machine vanished from sight once more, only a low mechanical moan signaling its departure.

"Do you think they were with the Mechanic?" Jade asked.

"Not sure, but there's only one way to find out." The shaking trees and trampled bushes provided the only clues for the bull to follow. The pod continued its trek across the light layer of snow until it reached a narrow hut with a thatched roof.

"This is it," Dan hissed. "The Mechanic's place."

"This can't be it," said Jade, peering over his shoulder. "There must be more."

The gears stopped whirring, and the smoke of the invisible machine faded away. The black-clad figures inside scrambled to the back of the machine, scooped up a bag full of mechanical parts, and shuffled inside the hut.

Dan and Jade left the bull in a thicket of bushes and crept toward the hut. Dan knocked twice. No one came to the door. Only the sounds of muffled shouts and rattling mechanical parts greeted them. Dan took a breath and banged on the door several times. "Hello? Is the Mechanic here?"

"Shhh," a rasping voice hissed from the other side. The door creaked open to reveal a small and frail dark-skinned man who leaned on a wooden crutch. "Keep it down, will you? They're already on my tail as it is?"

"Who?" Dan asked.

"Who are you children, and what are you doing at my door?"

"Well, good sir," said Jade, stepping forward. "My pod is in need of repairs, and Dan here is helping me with that. He is the grandson of Tarin and Gila."

"Oh, those two," he grumbled, throwing a sidelong glance at Dan, who blanched under the old man's gaze.

"As long as you can pay for new parts, and you don't cause too much of a ruckus, you can come in. But make it quick; you've already loitered at my door too long."

The old man swung the door open and gestured for them to come inside with a jerk of his head. It was dark inside the hut, with only a few dimly lit candles. The smell of grease clung to the room, although there were no signs of pods or tools. Loud snores greeted them as they passed the dining room. The Mechanic shook his head as he plodded toward a man lying slumped back on a wooden chair, his head lolling to the side as he snored softly, his gangly body splayed awkwardly over the chair.

"Jerry," the old man murmured, prodding the man in the side with his walking stick. When the snoring continued, the Mechanic banged his stick on the tiled wood floor. "Jeremiah!" he bellowed. "We have guests!"

"What?" Jeremiah woke with a start and he snapped to his feet, running a hand through his short blond ponytail. "Rosh, sir, I apologize! I was having a nap."

"A favorite pastime, I've noticed. Now, do you think you could lead the way to the workshop?"

Jeremiah replied with a salute, and he strode in front of the group and halted before a wall lined with two bookshelves that stood beside one another. He crossed his arms before spreading them out. A bolt of blue magic shot from palms and the two bookshelves shook before moving away from one another, uncovering a tall oak door. Jeremiah pushed the door open, revealing a large domed room.

"You can find anything you want here," said the Mechanic. They stepped out on to a raised platform with a railing and stairs on each side. Below were dozens of workers putting together pods of all kinds. They worked at kilns to create new parts, interlocked cogs, winding coils in mechanical limbs, and fusing on metal panels.

The back of the room was lined with shelves that displayed all kinds of mechanical legs and various other pieces. The legs, torso, and heads that could not fit on the shelves leaned against the stone walls. Dan gripped the railing at the front, his eyes darting about with rapt attentiveness.

"Invisibility shields aren't only for pods," explained Jeremiah. "Can't have the authorities snooping around this place. We just transferred the tech for the stealth setting on patrol pods and used it on the outside of this place. Took a while to figure out, but we got there."

"You look like you're about to burst, boy. Why don't you show him around, Jerry?" asked the Mechanic.

Jeremiah nodded and led Dan down the stairs to a small mechanical eagle whose back legs were missing.

"So, why is a noble coming to see a cranky old mechanic who's just scraping by?" said the Mechanic.

"How did you know I was nobility?"

"No commoner I've seen runs around with a patrol pod like that. That fancy way of talking doesn't help, either.

"It would be more convenient if I had a pod that didn't give away my station so easily. The legs are falling off my centipede. I need it to help me get out of this country."

"They weren't built to last for long treks in harsh weather. . You can see we have plenty. In fact, we just got a new collection of centipede parts."

"It's rare enough to be expensive, though. Might be an asset down the line. Things must be bad if you're surrounding yourself with people like us."

"I'm not popular with the others right now," Jade muttered.

"I've never been popular with 'em!" he said with a cackle. The Mechanic led them to a back door where the clanks and yells were coming from.

"I saw your crew collecting them from a noble's estate close by."

"You did, huh?" The old man scratched his bearded chin.

"You know that Earl never uses that thing? We asked him if we could haul that thing away for him. Told him people needed it, but he had us thrown out for trespassing.

"But why not let you take it if it isn't being used for anything?" Jade asked.

The Mechanic shrugged. "Nostalgia, status symbol; a little of both perhaps."

"But shouldn't you just leave it if that's what he wants?"

"You've seen what it's like out there," the Mechanic said, waving to the door behind him with his walking stick. "Not a thing will grow, and the markets are running out of supplies."

"And people will starve if they can't get to markets," Jade observed.

"Without a doubt. People need pods, and sturdy ones too. That's why I started this workshop. We're tryin' to make them accessible to people other than the higher-ups. You may not even count as one now, but you seem confident you can pay for this."

"Not a problem," Jade withdrew a sack full of coins from her robes and pressed it into the man's open palm. "Will this cover it?"

The man peered inside, and his eye grew large. "Good Spirits!" he exclaimed. "You can have anything you want and more for this! In fact, I'll even throw in a surprise!"

“Oh? Did you hear that, Dan? A surprise!” Jade shouted from over the rail, and Dan peered up at her, his grin growing even wider.

“What is this surprise?” Dan asked.

“I can’t just tell you what it is, can I? There’d be no fun in surprises then! Go join your friend and I call you when it’s ready!”

Jade and Dan stayed at the workshop until evening crept upon them, speaking with the workers and looking over the various parts. The Mechanic called for a break, and they ate a meal cooked by him and the crew. A few sat around his table, while others were scattered around the hut, casually discussing work and life.

A burly man walked by Jeremiah and snatched up a slice of cake, passing the tray as he fumbled to his feet and strode from the dining area.

“Why don’t you have more than a five-second break for once, Harlen?” Jeremiah asked.

“Machines won’t fix themselves,” mumbled Harlen before marching back into the workshop.

"This seems more like a community than a place of work," observed Jade.

"Old Rosh didn't just give us a job. He gave us a home when many of us were struggling to get by," said a woman who wore her long dark hair in a braided bun. She carried a lemon cake to the table and begin cutting slices. When she walked, the sound of creaking and whirring gears followed her.

"Sorry to pry, but what is that sound?" Dan asked.

"That's just Onya," said Jeremiah.

"We use machine parts for all kinds of things here," said Onya. She hiked up the leg of her tunic to reveal a leather binding around her right leg, with metal bracing keeping it in place.

The pair gaped in wonder. "There are more wonders here than magic can conjure," said Dan.

"You showed that you know your way around a pod, boy. Would you be interested in joining my crew?"

"Part of your crew? That would be an incredible experience. But I can't, my family needs me, I can't."

"You would be great," said Jade.

The others egged him on playfully.

As they grew progressively louder, he held his arms up and waved them down with a frown of mock indignation, his ears growing red. "Your enthusiasm is great, but for now, my answer is no."

The Mechanic shrugged. "It's your choice, but the position will still be here if ya ever change your mind."

Dan and Jade followed the routines of the crew until evening set in, and they waited, slumped in the dining room, eating leftovers of the lemon cake. Onya approached the pair in the workshop and told them to come with her.

"Here," said Onya when they arrived at the hut's entrance, waving a hand in front of her. The Atkins family's bull stood among the bushes. It gleamed in the dim evening light without a trace of rust, and a compartment filled with pod parts protruded from its back.

Dan and Jade reeled toward the machine to inspect it.

"Wait! What did you do?" said Dan, running his hands along the edges and peering inside. Several centipede pod legs were piled together, alongside parts for a centipede bull and various other types of parts all collected in a group. "You are all fantastic!" He almost started bouncing with joy.

Onya chuckled. "You're too kind. Rosh wanted you to have it."

The Mechanic hobbled to the pod. "You've got a great passion and eye for the craft. Make sure you continue with it."

"I will," Dan promised, running up to the man with open arms and scooping him up.

"Whoa," the Mechanic said as he backed away. "These bones are too old to take that."

"Sorry!" Dan loosened his grip and promptly placed the man back down. "Well, thank you," said Dan, holding out a greased hand.

The man shook the offered hand. "You can call me Rosh."

"We can fix the centipede pod so it will be better than new," Jade said with a sweeping bow.

"You can keep your bows, but I'm glad I could help you both. Just tell your Gran to be careful with her spells," he said and rubbed his rear end as if reliving a bad memory.

Dan and Jade chuckled and returned to the mechanical bull. It clopped along the pathway home with an ease and maneuverability that startled the pair.

"This runs so smooth even Miria would want to ride in this," Jade said with a snicker.

"There's far more room as well! We could fit many more people into this beauty."

The grinding of machine tracks echoed from behind them, and two heavy tanks halted before the hut. Dan and Jade exchanged frowns and turned the mechanical bull around, directing it away from the dirt road and deep into the nearby bushes. Dan brought the mechanical beast to a halt and shuffled from the pod. They snuck through the underbrush until they were close enough to see and hear the conversation taking place between the Mechanic and a broad-shouldered, stocky man flanked by two men with their spears held upright.

"Sir, I am the captain in these parts. The earl has made it clear on a number of occasions he did not want anyone touching his pod, yet several parts have gone missing from it over a long period. How do you justify this?"

"I'm just an old man trying to help those of us who can't afford to dump old pods on their property," said the Mechanic with a shrug.

The guards glared at the man. "Regardless, what you're doing is illegal," explained the captain.

"You are correct, sir," Onya said, stumbling forward and smiling in a placating manner.

"Who are you?" the captain demanded.

"Just one of the Mechanic's workers." She inclined her head slightly in a reverent gesture.

"Do you have the parts off of a patrol centipede?"

"Yes, yes, I do. He didn't know where they came from. It was all us. So please, good sirs, take us instead."

“What are you doing?” said the Mechanic. He shooed Onya back inside while the royal guards ignited spears and marched in the hut, pushing Onya to the ground.

Jade shot up from the grass and crossed her arms, throwing out a blast of magic in the air.

“It’s Sol’s daughter,” said one of the guards who stalked forward, his spear ignited.

“Aren’t I more interesting than them?” Jade asked, stepping toward the guards, her hands raised.

“Jade, what are you doing?” said Dan as he scrambled to his feet.

“Yes, you are far more interesting,” agreed the man as he gestured to the soldiers beside him.

Two men stomped forward and grasped Jade by the shoulders.

“What about your father? What about finding him?” Dan asked.

“I can save you all,” she said, her voice dropped to a whisper. “Besides, I’m practically a criminal now; they might send me to the Isle too.”

“I don’t know what you mean. Your father is dead, I’m afraid,” a guard informed her.

Jade’s face fell. “I know what I saw,” she whispered.

“He was executed, like every other traitor,” the captain explained matter-of-factly.

“Then why not dispose of a traitor publicly?” Dan demanded. “Is it because you’re secretly shipping people who don’t toe the line off to an island? Why would that be?” Dan took deep breaths to steady his nerves.

The clank of a spear as it fell to the forest floor was the only sound that filled the space. The Mechanic and his crew stood still, mouths agape.

“Is this true?” whispered the Mechanic. He turned to Jade. She froze, her voice locked in her throat. The guards handcuffed her and led her away by the shoulders to a tank.

Dan rushed forward. A guard swung a spear in front of his chest, halting the boy in his tracks. “I think you’ve done enough tonight, don’t you?” said the captain. “The boy is spouting nonsense. The Isle is a children’s story.”

"Sir," Onya began, "please let him go. None of this has anything to do with him."

"Stay out of this. He'll have to come with us now." The man jerked his head in the Mechanic's direction. Dozens of soldiers filed out of the tank, their spears ignited.

Onya turned to Dan. "Get behind us," she ordered. She and the rest of the crew gathered around him, whispering for him to leave.

"Take them all," the captain ordered, turning on his heel and marching back to a tank.

"Doesn't your word mean anything?" Jade pleaded.

The guards dragged the crew to their tanks and jabbed the tips of their electrified spears into the sides of anyone who tried to run. Jade's pleas for them to stop proved useless as the guards shoved her inside the tank along with the Mechanic's crew. Her eyes locked onto Dan's before the guards slammed the hatch with a thud. She stumbled about as the tank suddenly jerked. Screaming and thrashing echoed on the other side. Jade closed her eyes, trying to block out the terrified whisperings of the people huddled together in the dark, cramped space. She slumped onto the floor as the tank carried them down a long, winding road that led back to Rioda.

Chapter 5

Jade's eyes fluttered open, and she pushed herself up into a sitting position with a groan. She was greeted by the murmurings of the Mechanic's crew and the musty smell of their grease-covered clothes.

"What happened?" Jade asked as she fumbled into a sitting position.

"You're what happened," Onya muttered.

A man shot her a harsh glare. "If anything, we got you involved by stealing from nobles."

Jade shook her head. "I should have just given myself up long ago."

"Why would they be after a noble?" a man asked.

"It's complicated," Jade whispered.

"She's a troublemaker, that's why," a guard yelled from the front of the tank. "The whole family is made up of them."

The Mechanic's crew glared at her in confusion. Jade turned away, closing her eyes. Suddenly, a thought spiked in her tired mind and she jumped to her feet, stumbling to the front of the tank where the guards chatted casually and laughed.

"Is that why a dragon attacked my father's fiefdom out of nowhere?"

Their laughter came to an abrupt halt.

"What are you talking about?" Onya whispered.

"Her time on the run has made her delusional," the captain cackled, and the men continued their chatter as if she had never spoken. "Do you really think the nobility were behind a dragon attack?"

"They were always hoping for a way to get my father out of the picture. The dragon died from an attack by a guard before it could do too much damage, but he still chose to use his resources to rebuild, rather than the war effort, like they commanded him, too. It's almost like they were hoping he'd make that choice. The dragon didn't work, but now they had an excuse to demote and exile him."

"That sounds—" began a man sitting opposite her.

“I know,” said Jade, sliding a hand through her hair. “I know. I…I don’t even know what I believe anymore.” The rattling of the tank and the guards’ garbled laughter rang in Jade’s head like an off-key tune as she curled into a ball and fell into a dreamless sleep.

***

Their tank made regular stops at inns during the journey to Rioda, while the other tank continued traveling on to the capital. The guards allowed Jade and the Mechanic’s crew out for brief periods of time before they were ushered into the back of the cold and cramped metal tank. After the same grinding routine, they had all lost all sense of time, no longer knowing if they had traveled for days or weeks.

Jade was absently fiddling with the hem of her dress when their tank jolted to a stop. As they trudged outside, an inn nestled in the snowy landscape could be seen nearby. The sounds of a jaunty tune played on a violin filled the air. Jade closed her eyes, trying to shut out the memory of a small farm in the middle of nowhere.

The soldiers ordered them to move inside and made their way single file through the trembling door, held in place by one of the innkeeper's maids. Jade was flooded with warmth when she stepped inside, letting the temporary relief from the chilled air wash over her. They took a table at the farthest end and slid along its bench to sit. The maid plopped a bowl down in front of them before scurrying away into the back room with the other workers, exchanging nervous whispers and snatched glances as they watched the prisoners from a distance. A balding man in an apron hobbled past the maids with a ladle and a pot of lukewarm soup, serving up a portion of the thick yellow substance to each prisoner. They drank the soup in silence, always aware that multiple guards had their steely gaze fixed upon them.

"A poison only a witch could survive," mumbled a prisoner.

Jade winced at the old idiom.

When they had finished and a man bellowed at them to move out, Jade shuffled outside near the front of the line. Her gaze drifted across the snow-covered hills, the high and narrow towers of Rioda castle visible above the grey clouds. A cold dread gripped her heart.

As Jade took slow, labored steps up the ramp and into the back of the tank, the sound of metal scraping against wood pierced the air. Jade paused, her glance shooting behind her to where she heard the noise. The snow-laden forest was empty and silent once more.

"Stop dawdling," barked a guard, shoving her inside with the blunt end of his spear. She muttered an apology before trudging into the cold metal interior, Onya slumping down beside her before the hatch slammed shut.

"Here, you're looking a little too skinny there," said Onya as she snatched a bun from her robes and pushed it into Jade's hands.

"Where did you get this?"

"Bribed a guard. Had just enough denarans on me to get a couple of these. If I'd had more, maybe I could have bought my way out of here!" She threw her head back and barked out a dry laugh.

"Thank you, but I don't want it," Jade pushed it away, suddenly losing her appetite. She leaned back against the tank and wrapped her cloak tightly around her, trying to save the cold, as shivers ran through her body.

The sound of metal thrust against metal snapped Jade from her thoughts.

The tank slowed, and the guards cursed, demanding to know what was happening. Jade huddled close to the Mechanic's crew as a searing blue light pierced the hull, creating a circle. When the blue light completed the circle, a hand reached and discarded the broken metal. Miria gazed down at them with a crooked grin.

Chapter 6

"Miria!" Jade shouted. "How did you find me? Why would you come here? It took some searching in the eagle, and well, we're not here for the scenery, that's for sure. Come on, take my hand!" She reached down into the tank and extended her hand."

Jade held up her handcuffs. "But I can't…" Her voice faded away.

Miria leaned back, crossed her arms, and shot a beam of blue light at Jade's handcuffs. After the blue light engulfed them, they fell to the ground with a soft clank.

"Come," she said, reaching her hand down a little farther.

The tank jolted suddenly before grinding to a halt. Miria gripped at the side of the hole with one hand, almost falling inside. However, someone reached out from behind her, wrapping their arms around her waist and dragging her up.

A man Jade recognized from the Mechanic's crew peered down into the hole. "Hurry! I can't get all of you on board. I've got the boy at the controls, and the guards are already trying to get us off." His words were punctuated by the cries of the guards scaling up the side of the tank.

The Mechanic's crew gathered under the hole, their faces brightening as they threw dozens of questions at the man.

"We'll try to take as many of you as we can," Miria explained. "We…had an eagle. The bull's coming over, so get ready to hop in through the top hatch. Jade, hurry up!" Arrows flew around them. A persistent clank came from the side of the tank as a guard began climbing to the top.

"Take someone in my place," said Jade. "Make sure she leaves." She jerked her head toward the woman behind her.

"You need to find your father, remember?" said the woman.

"This is my best chance to do that," Jade protested. "They'll likely ship me off to the Isle with the rest of you."

The guard reached the top and tossed the man on the hull of the tank to the ground.

"Are you going to find him on their terms or yours?" said Miria. Guards approached her from behind, the tip of his electrical spear crackling. She managed to restrain one back with her magic, the tank shifting slightly to one side as he dangled from the edge. However, the other two kept advancing.

"No, please. Don't harm her!" Jade pleaded as the man ignored her. He lowered the spear, and it shot a wave of electricity through Miria's side, and she collapsed onto the tank's hull.

Jade cried out. She raised her head to meet the guard's gaze, her eyes ablaze with fury. The Mechanic's crew held her shoulders tight.

"Step back and take a deep breath before you do something you'll regret," Onya said in a hushed whisper. However, she pushed the crew aside and crossed her arms, releasing a shot of blue light up through the hole. The guard narrowly dodged it, fixing her with a furious glare. He held his spear by his side and prepared to jump inside the tank before someone grabbed him from behind and tackled him away from the hole.

"Help me up," Jade whispered.

The woman turned to the others. "Well, come on." The crew helped to boost Jade up to the hole. She gripped the sides and pulled herself up. Dan stood opposite the guard who was poised to attack. Jade rushed forward and pushed the guard to the ground. The man screamed as he hit the snow, grasping at his leg in pain. Jade gasped, her hands trembling. She took a deep breath and turned to Dan. They wrapped their arms around one another in a tight embrace.

"You got away?" said Jade.

"Thanks to what's left of the Mechanic's crew."

You came for me. I can't believe it."

"Neither could Miria." Dan turned his gaze toward his sister. They both shot to her side and helped lift her into a sitting position. Miria's eyes fluttered open.

"Are you all right?" Dan asked.

“Of course, I am.” Miria pushed herself into an upright position, holding her head. “So, you decided to join us topside?” she said with a tired smile.

“On our terms, right?”” Jade stood and held out a hand to Miria, who took it and rose to her feet.

“We’re waiting,” came a voice from below. They peered over the edge. The guards stood beside a dismembered pod in the shape of an eagle, its head and wings splayed across the snow-covered surface. They stood in a circle beside it. At the front of the group stood the man from the Mechanic’s crew. His face was distorted in anguish, and his wrists handcuffed behind his back, the guards’ electric spears buzzing behind him.

“I suggest you come down here now if you don’t want to make this situation even worse for you than it already is,” the guard standing directly behind the man warned.

Jade, Dan, and Miria exchanged nervous glances and descended the ladder on the tank’s side. The three stood in a row once they reached the surface and held up their hands. The guards held Dan’s and Jade’s shoulders with a firm and steady grip. Two guards stalked toward Miria, eyeing her blue pendant all the while, arms poised to snatch it up at a moment's notice. She backed away in long, arching movements, observing every twinge of their muscles with the care that a preyed upon animal took not to be consumed alive.

"Girl," said the captain, stepping in front of the men as they stood poised to strike. "Give us that magic stone, and we will work to gain you a pardon."

Miria crossed her arms, and a thin blue barrier rose between them. She shot the guards a threatening glare. "Let us go or I'll unleash all my powers!"

"Put that down now, witch," a guard barked, holding the tip of his crackling spear dangerously close to the barrier. "Don't do anything rash. Just back down like your other witch friend over there." He jerked his spear in Jade's direction.

"I'm no witch. I belong in the capital," whispered Jade, her voice hoarse from the cold.

Miria threw her a glare. However, she promptly turned her attention back to the guards. "Oh no. We're witches. I can command the weather, make changes, or even make the seasons stand still."

"Of course, you are all behind the weather," said the guard. "You're out to get us all, aren't you?"

Grains of snow fell atop Miria's open palms. "If one of us could make this happen, just imagine the damage that we can spread." She took a step forward, arms still crossed, and a crooked smirk across her face.

After a pause, the guard flicked his eyes across to the page restraining Dan. The page shoved Dan, making him fall into the snow and dirt. He held his spear over the young man's head.

"If you have anything resembling a human heart, then you'll give us that stone," said the captain.

Miria stared in silence, her expression blank. Finally, she lowered her hands, and the barrier dissipated. She removed her pendant and strode forward.

"Are you going to risk angering a witch?" said Dan, his fist digging into the snow until his knuckles were white, the sparks flying at his back. "You can take her pendant, and even cuff her hands, but she'll still have her powers. I don't want to think about what she and her friend here could do. What would the regent say if the capital were to collapse because you took a pair of powerful and dangerous witches prisoner?"

A long silence descended. "You have a lot of cheek, talking to us like that," said the head guard.

"I apologize, sir. I only speak the truth."

"Indeed," the man said, cocking his head. "A witch can always find a way. Let them go." He waved a hand toward the page.

"But, sir," the page protested.

"I said, let them go. We have enough going on with wild dragons. We don't need wild witches as well."

The page huffed in frustration, and sputtered something unintelligible, yet lowered his spear. The other guards followed suit.

The guards marched past them; two guards led the man from the Mechanic's crew into the tank. The back hatch creaked open, and the guards shoved him inside with the rest of the Mechanic's captured crew.

"Wait! Let them go! Please!" pleaded Jade.

The captain marched to the front of the tank. "You've won. I suggest that you leave and let us have this minor victory. Why fight for something that doesn't concern you?" he said with a firm shake of his spear, the electric tips softly crackling.

"Sir," muttered the guard who'd fallen from the tank. "We should take that." He gestured to the metal bull flickering in and out of visibility.

"You agreed to back away, now get back in your tank and leave," Miria growled.

"That is an excellent idea," said the captain. "You three! Go!" His gaze fell on the men and he brushed a hand toward the pod.

With a quick bow and a curt nod, they obeyed, making their way toward the pod and rummaging through the back tray. They shouted with joy while removing ropes, mechanical parts, and a first aid kit.

"I told you to back away," Miria barked. She released a beam of blue light that snipped through the branch of an ash tree. The fallen branch made the guards jump back in fright.

"If you won't give us the stone, then you can't expect us to just walk away with nothing." The injured guard rose to his feet with the help of two others who stood on either side of the man. The guard continued, "Our forces might be limited now, but we'd have a duty to call in more forces and stop you…unless you give us an offering. An assurance you'll leave us and everyone else in peace."

Miria kept her stance, turning her gaze to her two companions. Jade tried to stifle a series of coughs and wrapped her arms around herself, looking as though she wanted to collapse into the snow.

Dan brought his hands to his face, blowing on them to stave off the cold. He panted heavily and appeared weak and defeated. Miria trembled from both rage and the searing cold. She lowered her arms. "All right," she whispered.

"All right?" repeated the head guard.

"You can have the thing. We'll be on our way and never cause you trouble again."

"Excellent!" said the head guard. "Now we can return home with the assurance that you will not harm us again. Please make all of this stop soon." He raised his head to the small drops of snow lightly raining down. The guards promptly stepped away from Dan and Jade, and they began their journey back to Rioda, tank roaring downhill, accompanied by the canter of the fully visible mechanical bull.

The three stared at one another in shocked silence. Dan's fists trembled as his gaze traveled to the scattered pieces of the mechanical eagle. "What are we going to tell the Mechanic's crew?"

"The truth?" said Miria. "There was nothing we could do." She turned on her heel, took a breath, and stalked toward Jade. "Are you hurt?"

Jade shook her head. She wrapped her cloak around her shoulders, her eyes drawn and her voice barely above a whisper. "But I'm tired. And I've eaten nothing but tavern slop for…I don't even know how long."

“Well then, we’d better put this bird back together. Dan, get the tools out of the back.” She snatched up screws and parts that were strewn across the snow.

“Where’s the Mechanic and the others?” Jade asked, her gaze falling on Dan.

“They gave up a lot to make sure I got away safe,” said Dan, his eyes downcast. “Too much. I couldn’t even fix the centipede with all of this going on,” He waved to the broken eagle pod.

“You put yourself in unnecessary danger for me.” Jade swept a bow in a gesture of thanks. She fought the sudden urge to laugh at how out of place and stiff the motion seemed in the vast, empty woods. Jade promptly straightened and gathered her cloak tight around her chest as a shiver ran through her spine.

“It was necessary,” said Miria with a slight shrug while shuffling to Jade’s side. “Dan begged me. Gran and Pa nearly had a fit after you left.”

“Elisa will be thrilled,” said Jade, rolling her eyes. The ghost of a smile tugged at the corner of her lips. After a silence, the three broke into soft, awkward chortles.

Their laughter was interrupted by Jade's sudden violent coughing and shivering. Miria rushed to her side.

"We'd better get out of here," said Dan. He moved to the mechanical bird and poked around until he withdrew a leather pouch lined with tools.

Jade closed her eyes. "I'm still no closer to the Isle than I was when I started this journey. , We'll talk about that later. You're in no condition to travel right now," said Miria.

A rasping cough arose from Jade's chest again as she shook her head. "I'm fine," she said before releasing another series of coughs.

"We have different definitions of fine. Come on, I'll make us a fire." Miria began collecting pieces of old wood. "Go sit over there," she said, flicking her fingers toward a nearby log. Jade nodded and made her way to the log, barely listening to the brief chatter exchanged between brother and sister before the pieces of wood were littered in a pile in front of her and set alight with a wave of Miria's arms. Jade closed her eyes, and the warmth brought a sense of clarity that she'd never felt before.

"You were right," Jade whispered when Miria sat beside her on the log.

"You'll have to be more specific," she said, choking out a mild chuckle and offering Jade a crooked smile. When she met Jade's dour gaze, her smile fell a little, and she waited for her companion to continue.

"Maybe he's gone forever," Jade murmured. "He could be somewhere sitting by a fire, just like this. But he's on an island with no way off. Not unless you're one of them." Jade locked her gaze onto the tall thin spires of Rioda castle, a beacon of strength designed to ward off all enemies.

"Why?" Miria demanded.

Jade blinked in confusion.

"Why are they the only ones who can let people in and out, as if they owned it?"

"That's just how things are. Maybe you were right, and it might as well be a fairy tale to the rest of us."

"On your own terms, remember? My parents didn't make it, but I'm making sure you do."

"I can't ask you to do that," said Jade.

"You're not! I'm volunteering."

"You have a good life on the farm. You shouldn't ruin that."

Miria gazed into the fire, about to speak, when Dan took a seat beside her on the log. He held out his broad, calloused hands in front of the fire for warmth. "There are still more parts lost in the snow. I'll get back to it in a moment," he murmured.

"I'll help. Rest first, we can't rush anything if we want to get home in one piece," said Miria.

"I've done a lot of thinking," said Jade.

"Don't imagine you've had much else to do," said Miria. She pressed a hand to the other girl's shoulder.

"What if someone else got a hold of something like that?" Her gaze rested on Miria's glowing pendant.

"I doubt it," said Dan. "They'd need to get it from the Isle."

"They seemed interested in yours," said Jade.

"They need to go find their own jewelry," Miria scoffed. "But Dan's right. This was brought to our world from the other realm. You don't see them every day."

"If they can reach the Isle, maybe they can reach more," Jade mused.

Miria chewed her lip, her expression settling into grim thoughtfulness. "You don't think the dragon that attacked your dad's fiefdom…" She let the implication of that statement linger between them.

"I don't know," said Jade, collecting brittle sticks that protruded from the snow and flicking them into the fire.

"My family's studied dragons for generations. They understand more about them than most ever will," said Miria.

"I really have been on the run for too long," Jade muttered. "It's doing my head in."

"I'm sure you'll find the answers you're looking for on the Isle," said Dan. He tossed a twig into the fire. Laughing birds and the crackling fire were the only sounds that filled the forest.

“What has Avi been up to?” Jade asked.

“Eating everything he can,” said Dan with a chuckle. “He does that when he’s worried.”

“That kid’s been missing you,” added Miria.

A smile flashed across Jade’s face. “Then I suppose we should all get back to the farm,” she said in a low, tentative voice. They rested by the fire until their strength returned.

Chapter 7

Dan flicked a series of switches, and the metallic bird whirred back to life. Jade and Miria pushed the pod through the snow before crawling inside the bottom hatch. Miria scrambled inside and hooked an arm around her brother's waist while extending her other arm out toward Jade. Racing to keep up with the pod, Jade grasped the offered hand and climbed inside. She turned and grasped for the handle of the back hatch as it flapped in the wind and yanked it shut. They panted while settling into the cramped space that reeked of grease and sweat.

Miria's short round arms wrapped around her brother's middle, squeezing in a near bone-crushingly tight manner, shutting her eyes and muttering curses.

"I think your brother will need to breathe if he's going to steer this bird," said Jade, biting her lip to restrain a chortle.

"Oh," Miria said, clearing her throat before loosening her grip. "Sorry."

The forest became a green and white blur as the mechanical eagle raced through the sky, and the wind whistled as the metal panels softly rattled. The tin roof of the Mechanic's hut stood out among the trees, patches of snow decorating the domed workshop's invisible surface. Dan steered the pod to the east, moving the machine toward a clearing. While easing the mechanical eagle downward, its right wing brushed against a tree and flew away, setting the pod off balance. He pulled at the wheel and the machine collided with the ground, gliding through the snow in a circle before coming to an abrupt stop.

Dan let out a sheepish chuckle, "Sorry. But not too bad for a first landing. You doing all right, Miria?"

She responded by moving past him and crawling out of the eagle's open mouth. "This is why I hate pods," she mumbled.

Dan and Jade followed her out of the pod. They took a moment to stretch their legs and adjust to the surface.

Dan turned to the pod with a sigh. "Come on, we'd best get to the workshop. We can't exactly drag it back in our condition." He removed his cap and wrung it tight in swift, erratic motions while they trudged through the snow single file to the workshop.

"You're not going to the gallows, brother. Just tell them it was my fault. I'll accept it," said Miria.

"I just wish we'd put more effort into saving at least one more member."

"You can't save everyone, Dan."

Jeremiah emerged from the bushes, followed by Harlen, who carried the metal piece that had split from the mechanical bird during their landing.

"Why don't you just go to the guards yourself and tell them we're still here?" said Harlen, waving the wing's tip in front of them.

"I was careless," said Dan, gripping his cap tighter.

"Where's the bull?" Jeremiah asked.

"Look." Dan ran a hand through his messy brown hair. "I have no excuse."

"There was nothing we could do," said Miria. She stepped beside her brother and met the men's gaze with a quiet ferocity.

"It was a lost cause from the start," Jeremiah said. "At least you got your friend."

"Where is everyone else?" Jade asked.

"Gone," said Harlen. He hauled the metal piece over to where the pod was and began reattaching it.

"We're all that's left," Jeremiah explained.

"The guards took everyone? And we couldn't even bring back the others," said Jade.

"Who are you and why did you come to our workshop?" Jeremiah eyed Jade, rubbing his greasy hands against his shirt.

"That's none of your business!" Miria snapped.

"The boy said something about a secret convict system. If that's true, then it's all of our business."

Jade nodded. "I'm trying to find my father. I think they took him to the Isle of Dragons."

"The Isle?" Harlen crossed his arms, stifling a bemused chuckle.

"It's real," said Dan. "Who knows? Maybe that's where they'll take your friends."

"You know how this sounds, don't you?"

"Regardless of how it may sound, it's still true," said Miria.

"I'll free them when I make it," Jade promised with a low bow.

The two men gawked at one another in disbelief.

"It's a wonder you're still with us, Jade of House Sol," Miria said, barely suppressing a bemused chuckle.

"It's admirable though," said Dan. He slumped his shoulders and yawned. "We'd best be getting home. We have a long walk ahead of us."

"Wait," said Jeremiah. He stomped in front of them, blocking their path. "You kids aren't sane, but you tried to get our crew back. That means something.." He shot Harlen a quizzical look. "Why don't we give them the bull?"

"But we hardly have anything now, Jerry."

"It's what the boss would want. Besides, it's not like we'll get any use out of it."

"Fine," he said, pointing to Dan. "But only if you keep workin' on your skills."

"Not sure I can do anything more. The bird still fell to pieces too easily when the guards came for it."

The two men exchanged tired looks before leading them to through the hut. After Jeremiah separated the bookshelves, they entered the barren workshop. A mechanical bull stood alongside another eaglelike pod with a rounder design.

"That was a prototype. Not as aerodynamic as the final product," Dan explained, the corners of his mouth quirking into a slight smile.

"Come here," Harlen waved him over to a worktable lined with blueprints, and Dan trotted behind him. He gathered a handful of papers together in a greasy palm and handed them to Dan. "The Mechanic had high hopes for you. We'll have to find jobs somewhere else, so a lot of these projects need to go on hold for now. But see how you go with this one."

Dan flicked through them, his eyes widening. "There's a lot of work here!"

"Yeah, and years of it."

Dan folded the papers and tucked them into his clothes.

"I'll do what I can."

"Good lad, now help us with this." Harlen turned on his heel and pointed to the pod draped in a large dirty brown sheet. They pulled the cover off the machine, a mechanical bull resting underneath. It was smaller than the previous one, with patches of rust adorning its horns and back.

"It was one of our pet projects before this mess," said Jeremiah. "This isn't a patch on the one we modified for you, but it's all we could do with just us."

"It's not so bad," laughed Dan. "A little more polish and she'll be fine. We won't forget this."

“Another pod,” Miria groaned. “Well, at least it’s better than walking in the snow.” She marched behind Jade and Dan while they climbed in through the bull’s side hatch. “At least we’re not walking home.”

Harlen punched a button on the wall, and gears cranked and groaned as the workshop’s back door rolled open. After saluting the men, Dan made the mechanical beast rise, and a gust of snow hit the pod before it bolted from the workshop and into the forest.

“Has Elisa been snooping in my room?” Jade asked. She shivered as the winds whistled through the cracks in the drafty metal bull.

“We’re nearly there. We’re nearly there,” Miria recited, her arms wrapped tightly around Jade’s waist, ignoring her question.

Jade chortled. She leaned her head against Dan’s back and closed her eyes. *It’s almost like going home,* she thought.

Chapter 8

Several days passed in relative quiet, with Miria and Dan helping Jade to plot out a route to Marda while she recovered from her sickness. Elisa complained about getting used to a different and less efficient bull to anyone who'd listen. The smaller and creakier bull was harder to maneuver than the newly upgraded one.

One morning, the family was gathered around a map when a loud persistent knocking came at the door. Jade sat up, collected the map in her arms, and peered through the window to get a look at who was summoning them. Riley stood outside the cottage, flanked by several guards.

"They're here for me." A guard turned his gaze to the window, and Jade ducked under the table.

"You go hide upstairs, and we'll handle this," said Tarin.

Gila nodded.

Elisa shifted about uncomfortably in her seat, opening her mouth to speak. However, she remained silent.

Jade raced upstairs, leaning against a wall so she was out of sight but still in earshot of the goings-on downstairs. She covered her mouth to suppress her coughs. Tarin and Gila rose, nodding to one another.

"No matter what happens, you stay here," Gila told her grandchildren before hobbling to the front door with Tarin.

Tarin opened the door halfway. "Good morning! How may we help you, young man?" He greeted the soldiers with a jovial grin and wrapped an arm around Gila.

The young man tipped his hat and smiled. "Hello, my name is Riley Johnson and I'm with the King's Guard. I was wondering if you'd seen a missing girl. She'd be riding a big machine. It's a massive centipede. Have you seen anything like that?"

Jade peeked over the banister. Riley now wore the gold insignia that Kaylen once displayed on her uniform.

Gila and Tarin looked to one another before turning back to the man, shaking their heads. "No, can't say we have. But may I ask why you're looking for this girl?" Tarin asked. Jade leaned in a little closer.

“Her father is also missing, and she’s gone searching for him. We’ve all been worried sick about her.”

Jade rolled her eyes.

“He heard that she was last seen in a nearby forest and asked if we could help. We’ve been going around each house in the neighborhood,” Riley continued.

“We are awfully sorry to hear that. If we should see her, we will contact the authorities immediately,” Gila said and reached for the door handle. Riley jammed his hand inside the door, pushing it wide open, his genial smile never wavering.

“Pardon me, but we would like to have a look inside if you don’t mind.” The men prepared to enter the household when Tarin stood in their way, holding his arms out.

“Actually, we do mind. We’d prefer it if you left now,” Tarin said as he stared the man down. Riley casually brushed Tarin aside with a wave of his arm, knocking him to the floor. Jade shot up from her position behind the banister. Gila threw her a disapproving look, gesturing for her to stay with a slight flick of her walking stick. Jade remained fixed in place.

"Pa!" Elisa rushed to her grandfather's side, helping him to his feet.

Before the guardsman could take another step, Gila crossed her arms and raised them to the young man's chest. They shot out a ball of light at the soldiers, narrowly missing them. The guardsmen halted, gaping at the old woman who held her cane directly in front of them.

"I'll ask you to leave one last time. Please keep in mind that if you take one more step inside this house, I promise that I won't miss a second time."

The men drew their spears, the tips beginning to sizzle.

"What is this?" Riley demanded. "I could have you tried for witchcraft!"

"I highly doubt that, young man," Gila said with a self-assured smirk.

Dan rose from his seat, about to move to the door, followed by Miria.

Jade crept from her hiding spot and leaned over the banister. “Psst, Miria.”

She motioned for the other woman to come up with a flick of her hand. Miria rushed up the steps, and Jade shuffled toward her, whispering in her ear. Miria’s lips curved into a wry grin. She unfastened the stone from around her neck and pressed it into Jade’s hands.

“I can do this,” Miria assured, rushing down the staircase.

“Wait,” Elisa pleaded in front of Gila. “Maybe we can come to some agreement.”

“Finally, someone here who speaks sense!” Riley deactivated his spear, sliding it into a leather sheath behind his back. “Why don’t you let us inside for a moment, and then you won’t have any more worries. I can make it worth your while,” he said, jangling a satchel of coins in front of her.

“I…” Elisa took a step back. Her eyes darted from Riley to her grandparents, who shook their heads vigorously. Elisa froze.

"Sir, I must apologize for my grandparents," Miria interrupted, wedging herself between Riley and Elisa. "This is all an unfortunate misunderstanding. I have the information you seek!"

The young man folded his arms, raising a brow, "Oh?"

"I believe I've spotted the girl you're looking for." Gila lowered her stick, throwing her oldest granddaughter a quizzical look. "Not that long ago, I was visiting friends in a village you would have just passed. I saw the outline of a huge, metal centipede, crawling through Nearwood Forest," Miria said while gesturing wildly.

"Nearwood Forest?" repeated Riley, cocking his head in curiosity.

"The villagers have seen the centipede," Miria assured. "She went down a hill close to a duke's estate."

Riley placed a hand on his chin and considered her words. Silence filled the air until Riley finally waved the men back, his expression blank.

"Thank you for your help," he said and stepped back, his gaze fixed on Miria and her grandparents all the while. “Oh, before we go, would you happen to have seen a glowing blue stone?”

“I don’t have the faintest idea what you’re talking about,” Miria said with a shrug. “Sorry.”

“All right. Thank you.” he said with the flicker of a smile. “We won’t forget this.” Riley and his guards marched from the property and out of sight.

When Miria closed the door, Gila lowered her stick and, leaning on it, she melted into a low chuckle. “What was that?”

“I don’t think diplomacy is for me, Jade!”

Jade made her way down the stairs. “Are you all right, Tarin?”

“It’ll take more than a small nudge like that to harm me. He gave me a bit of a scare, though,” Tarin said. Dan guided him to his place at his rocking chair, lighting the old man’s pipe.

“Not bad, Jade of House Sol,” said Miria.

"Throwing your opponents off your trail is a trick you have to master on the run and in court," said Jade. Her voice trailed off as her gaze followed the retreating guards.

Gila cackled, "I like you, girl! Well done, but I think it would be best to put up a barrier with our magic in case they come knocking again. It will take several days, and I'll need help."

Jade held her arm, shamefaced. Before she could say anything, Gila hobbled toward her. "Remember, you're here because we want you to be. I've taken on a hundred of those bloated fools at once, and I'll do it again if I must." Miria, Dan, and Avi nodded.

Elisa turned her gaze from the others.

"Elisa," Jade said, approaching the younger girl and grasping her shoulder. Elisa pulled away from Jade's touch, eyes downcast.

"What were you doing? You could have got us all in trouble! You know you can't trust the guards as far as you can throw them!" Gila said, turning to her youngest granddaughter.

“She was just scared,” said Jade. “Everyone makes mistakes when they’re scared.”

“True enough,” Gila conceded, “I almost forget how young you are sometimes. Just…try to keep your wits about you next time. All right, girl?” Gila’s tone softened.

Elisa nodded. She turned and trudged up to her room while Dan and Avi made their way back to the kitchen.

“This never would have happened back in Nyonan,” Gila mumbled as she hobbled to Tarin’s side.

“But this country has more of us,” Tarin said between smoking his pipe as if recalling an old, familiar conversation. They shared a knowing grin.

Jade turned to Miria and frowned. “That was easy. Far too easy.”

“The whole thing went a little too smoothly,” Miria agreed. A sense of foreboding clasped Jade’s heart as her gaze followed the guards’ retreating backs.

“Maybe I should—” Jade began.

“Just relax,” said Miria. “We won’t let anything happen. Go upstairs and get some rest.”

Jade nodded, offering a forced smile.

***

That night after dinner, Gila rose from her place at the table and limped to the front door.

“All right, you lot,” she said, gesturing to Jade, Miria, and Avi. “Night is always the best time to put up a barrier. It’s when the connection between our realm and the other is strongest.”

“Are you sure you can do this Jade?” asked Tarin.

“The barrier will be stronger the more people help. Besides, My head’s already starting to clear, thanks to your brew.”

“We’ll be straight in and out,” said Gila.

“But it’s still too cold,” Avi complained.

“It’s always cold now, Av,” Dan said with a good-natured grin and a playful shove. “It will be worse for Jade.”

The four magic users marched outside single file behind Gila, with Avi and Jade wrapped in a thick coat.

Gila turned to face the three and cleared her throat. "We will stand in a circle around the farm, hold out our hands on either side of us, concentrating all our energies on protecting this home…and utter complete nonsense."

"What?" asked Jade, certain she'd heard that last part wrong.

"You only have to chant something. It doesn't matter what it is," Gila explained.

Jade still regarded the old woman with complete befuddlement.

Gila held her stick out at Jade. "This is a way to channel your magic, to focus it. Words are a way to amplify it."

"I feel a little ridiculous, just muttering nonsense."

"From what you've told us, that seems to be all your friends in the capital ever do," observed Gila.

"You have a point," Jade said with a bitter laugh.

"Of course, I do. If you have a voice, use it. Now spread out, kids!"

They all found somewhere to stand around the cottage, so that they formed a circle. Jade crossed her arms and held her palms up to the chilled air. She closed her eyes, trying to shut out Avi's babbling. Thinking back to her old life, a tune danced across her memories until she began to hum what her mother had called "The Cricket Song" in a slow, soft rhythm.

The song called forth images of night's by the fire, her mother softly humming while pouring over a book, while her father carved out toy dragons.

She took a breath and cracked open an eye. A sparkling white and blue sheet of magic spread over the farm, creating a large, semitransparent dome.

Jade smiled, her shoulders dropping in exhaustion. Gila approached the magic dome, ran a hand over it, and then lightly knocked on it a couple of times.

"Sturdy," she mumbled. "You all put strong intent into it. Good job," she said with a yawn. Everyone appeared drained, with Avi nearly falling asleep on his feet. Jade coughed.

"Sorry to get you out here in the condition you're in, but I needed your help," said Gila. "Come on, girl. Let's get you inside and huddled up by the fire."

Jade trudged behind them.

"Magic is the best kind of strange, isn't it?" said Miria, slowing her pace to match hers.

Jade set her gaze up to the night sky, her mind drifting faraway. "Please tell Dan to hurry with the repairs."

***

No one set foot on the Atkins property again. The translucent blue barrier made an interesting spectacle that drew the interest of passers-by. Jade and the others would go out now and then and use their magic to maintain the barrier and keep it strong.

Jade spent her time sitting in her room, a shawl wrapped around her shoulders, and drinking the cough brew Gila and Tarin brewed for her. Her strength was gradually returning, and her cough had nearly left her entirely. A map, scattered denaran coins, and a rough sketch of her pod were splayed across her bed. She counted each coin repeatedly, rubbing the sleep from her eyes as she muttered each number under her breath. She had still had many denarans, but not enough to buy another pod. Jade held up the drawing of the centipede she had. A girl traveling alone in a patrol pod reserved for the Royal Guard would raise too many questions. But even if she sold the pod, no amount of money would be enough for a crew to agree to sail her to the Isle and back again.

"Time to eat," Elisa's voice snapped Jade from her thoughts.

"Coming!" Jade descended the stairs and clapped along as Dan played his fiddle, her mind always drifting to the map upstairs. Before she could excuse herself, a deep, a pained howl cut through the winter night, interrupting the evening dance.

"What is that?" Dan asked while tucking his violin back in its case.

"I have no idea. It doesn't sound like any beast I've ever heard," muttered Miria, placing a hand to her chin.

“It sounds like a banshee or a ghost,” Avi observed.

“Those things don’t exist,” Elisa corrected her younger brother.

“Will the barrier keep it out?” Jade asked.

“The barrier only works for those not connected to the realm of magic,” Gila explained.

“I think I’ve heard that sound before,” said Jade, a tremble in her voice. Her eyes grew wide and hollow as she desperately hoped she was wrong.

“Our Miria can handle it, whatever it is,” Dan said, leaning back in his chair.

“True, and there’s no use staying up worrying. We’d all best get some sleep,” said Tarin.

Everyone voiced their agreement. However, the brief glances they all exchanged carried a quiet sense of dread.

Jade fought the whispers of sleep, staring up at the ceiling, her hands clasped tight. The creaks and moans of the cottage kept Jade alert as the pained cries echoed in the distance. As the night drew on, the wailing grew close, piercing the chilled night air. Jade bolted upright and scrambled to the window, her eyes widening in fear. :a towering pale dragon scoured the village, setting homes aflame. She dashed into the hall where she met Miria, who hastily threw on a shawl and fastened the stone pendant around her neck, her flute poking from the front pocket of her robes.

"I saw it," Jade panted. "It's like the one that attacked my home!"

Miria pressed her hands on Jade's shoulders. "I'll do what I can, okay?"

Jade could only nod, her eyes fixed on the wooden floorboards.

"All right. Let's go," said Miria, and they both hurried outside.

Just beyond the farm, the towering pale dragon writhed about, seemingly in pain, eyes white and unfocused. The creature howled in a strangled, unnatural manner as it spat fire. Houses and barns were ablaze. People and animals galloped away in a panicked haze, while others gathered together to fight the fires as best they could by piling on snow, tossing buckets of water, or damping down the flames with old rags.

Dan shot outside, pulling on a pair of boots as he stood beside the pair. “I’ll help put out the fires. Miria, be careful approaching that thing!”

Miria took a breath and stepped forward.

Jade intended to help put out the fires yet froze in place. Her gaze fixed upon the thin, writhing monster before her. Images of a night filled with the same cries filled her mind. The dragon’s blank white eyes settled on Dan and the crowd of men and women putting out the fires, and it stalked toward them.

Miria approached the dragon, the stone’s light shining in its hollow pale eyes. The beast shook off the light and stomped past her. She followed the creature’s movements in quiet shock as she fumbled for her flute. As she began to play, the creature let out a banshee screech, whipping it from her hands with a swipe of its long tail. The dragon turned its hulking body to face Miria. The beast’s glare and rage found a target and it bounded forward, crushing the flute in its claw. Miria's eyes widened in terror and she backed away.

The Atkins family gathered outside the farmhouse. They clung to one another and watched with screams of horror as the beast advanced toward Miria, releasing a plume of flames. She scrambled away, narrowly dodging the fire. The beast backed her up against the crumbling ashen barn wall. Miria trembled, eyes darting about frantically.

Jade willed herself forward, running toward Miria, the growling creature blocking her way.

Dan stopped tending to the fire. "Miria!" He ran to her. A man held him back, yelling "You'll just get yourself killed along with her."

Jade shut her eyes tight, crossed her arms, holding her trembling palms up to the sky.

"Please," she whispered. She vanished into the night air, blue magic engulfing her body. The magic transported her to Miria's unconscious form. Jade hoisted the other woman up into her arms and dragged her from the flames, gasping in pain as the fire burned her side. They both fell to the ground. The snow numbed her side somewhat.

Unsteadily, Jade pushed herself to her feet to face the dragon. She picked up a rock to use as a makeshift weapon with the Atkinses also preparing rocks and sticks in case it approached. However, the beast trembled, its legs giving way, and it fell to the snow, unmoving. Panting from fear and exhaustion, Jade turned to inspect the damage. The family hovered over Miria's unconscious body, her right arm seared red and black.

Chapter 9

Jade refused to move from Miria's bedside. Dan took the mechanical bull to fetch the nearest doctor. There were thick bandages around Jade's torso that Gila applied until the doctor could inspect her and Miria's wounds.

"Starving yourself won't help either of you," Gila said in a raw, scratchy voice. She placed a tray of bread and water on the dressing table and brushed a hand against Jade's shoulder. She leaned heavily on her walking stick and let out an exhausted breath. After helping Jade, Gila had lowered the magic barrier for the doctor.

"You should never have let me into your home." Jade's voice was cracked and distant.

"We don't know why this happened. No one blames you; least of all, Miria."

"You don't know that," Jade mumbled into her intertwined fingers.

"I know that you can't take everything on your shoulders," Gila said and hobbled from the room, closing the door behind her with a soft click.

Jade's gaze remained on Miria. "I'm sorry," she murmured.

Silence filled the Atkins home. Elisa stayed in her room with the door shut, refusing to come out. Tarin and Gila waited in the kitchen, stone-faced and exhausted until the door flew open and Dan rushed in with the physician by his side. They scrambled to their feet and rushed to greet them.

"You have no idea how good it is to see you, James," said Gila.

The man held a bag of supplies under one arm, and he reached out to shake their hands with the other.

"Gila, Tarin, I am so sorry. Take me to her now."

"She's right this way," said Tarin. He ushered the man up the stairs to Miria's room.

When he entered, Jade was snapped from her thoughts, leaping to her feet. "Doctor!"

His gaze traveled over her with a sigh and shook her hand. “You’ve both been through a lot. I will be with you as soon as I’ve seen to Miria.”

Jade gave a quick bow before shuffling from the room and treading softly down the stairs to where Dan stood by the fireplace, his back facing her. He pressed a hand onto the mantelpiece while staring into the flames.

She stepped toward him and reached out a hand, about to speak. However, her thoughts were too chaotic to form the words she needed. Instead, she began to pace up and down the carpet, lost in her thoughts once again as the muffled sounds of the physician echoed softly from upstairs.

“This wasn’t your fault,” Dan mumbled, his back still turned to her as he shifted logs about in the fireplace with a poker.

“So, I keep hearing,” said Jade.

“At least you could do more than put out fires.” He continued to stare into the fire.

“What? You’re the reliable one here, Dan. This was all a mistake,” muttered Jade. “I’d best wait for the doctor.”

Before he could reply, she made her way up to her room, throwing herself onto the bed. She gazed blankly up at the ceiling until she heard a soft rapping on her door.

"The doctor's finished now." It was Tarin. "Miria." He paused. Jade held her breath. "She's going to be all right," he said at last. She sighed.

"The doctor's coming to see you too, okay?"

The door creaked open, and the man whisked inside. "Excuse me, miss? May I sit down?"

Jade pushed herself up, swinging her legs over the side of the bed. She gestured to the chair beside her bed.

"Thank you," he said, taking a seat and inspecting her side.

"You know, young Dan told me what you did tonight. I'm old friends with Tarin and Gila, so I just want to thank you on their behalf."

"Please don't say that," said Jade. "I've only been a burden to them since I arrived."

"From what I can gather, they don't feel that way. I've known the Atkins family a long time, well enough to know they would think no such thing."

"How's Miria?" whispered Jade.

"As best as we could have hoped for," the doctor replied as he busied himself checking Jade's wounds. Silence filled the room.

When the physician had finished treating her, he picked up his bag and walked to the door. "When Dan showed up in a large, elegant machine that's only found in the capital, I had questions. However, there were more urgent matters at hand. He only said that he'd borrowed it from a friend. I don't know who you are or why you are here, but you have the Atkins family's trust, and that is enough for me. Please make sure you get rest." He tipped his hat, then left the room, closing the door softly behind him. Jade turned to the window, snow clinging to the windowsill. She closed her eyes.

After the physician said goodbye to Gila and Tarin, he left with Dan in the metal centipede.

Jade spent the rest of the evening locked away in her room, perched on her bed, eyes wide open and her knees drawn up to her chest. The white-eyed dragon and Miria's arm appeared every time she closed her eyes. When the centipede pod roared into the work shed and Dan returned to the house, she pushed herself from the bed and began pulling the drawers loose, stuffing her belongings into her knapsack. After collecting all of her things together, she slung the knapsack over her shoulder. She waited until Dan stomped up to his room before dashing down the stairs and into the cold night air. Jade dashed inside the mechanical centipede, switched on the engine, and flashed on the stealth setting. The invisible mechanical creature took off into the chilled winter night.

The metal creature still blinked in and out of sight; Dan was still working on repairing the stealth mode. Its creaks and whirs rang loudly in Jade's ears. She ignored its poor condition andmaneuvered the pod through valleys and over winding hills until the Atkins farm was far behind her. She stayed clear of any townships and traversed through forests instead. She planned to venture into populated areas only for essentials and to find a mechanic who would repair her pod with no questions asked. A dim light shone far in the distance; Jade made out the outline of another, much larger pod relentlessly marching in her direction.

She pulled a lever, increasing the speed. The other pod wasn't fast, but it was strong and large, continuing to plow through the snow with determined strides. As she guided the mechanical beast over a snow-covered log, the centipede's legs stiffened, moving about in slow, jerking movements until they collapsed under the mechanical beast.

"Damn it," Jade hissed between her teeth. The other pod grew closer. She wildly pulled at levers and pressed buttons to no avail. She took in a deep breath, trying to calm her breathing. She let out a ragged breath, eyes darting to the approaching pod. The centipede jolted as the incoming machine rammed into Jade's pod just hard enough to tip the centipede on its side without doing severe damage.

Jade peered out of the opening of her pod. A rusted old bull stood before her.

"Dan?" she shouted and stumbled from the centipede's mouth, shielding her eyes from the light. "What are you doing here?"

The hatch fell open, and Elisa rushed out, her eyes filled with tears and rage. “So, you’re just going to walk out on us? After all that?” she demanded, weakly pushing Jade, who stumbled back slightly.

“Elisa? What are you doing here?”

“What do you think? Bringing you home.”

“But, the dragon! Miria! It was all my fault.”

“Miria would be dead if it wasn’t for you.”

“I can’t go back. You were right! I should never have involved you all!” Jade closed her eyes and took a deep breath. She had tried to outwit nobility twice her age but had neither the experience nor wits to win against them. She now believed that she was merely a guest who’d intruded on people who were too generous and led danger to their doorstep. All she could do was run. “I need to do this alone.”

“You really have a death wish, don’t you?” said Elisa, shoving Jade by the shoulders again. The younger girl glared at her with a mixture of anger and weariness.

Jade turned away from Elisa, wrapping her arms around herself and glancing at her pod. “Why are you even here? You wanted me to leave more than anyone.”

“I was wrong, okay?” said Elisa “I can’t remember anything but Miria being there for us. When you showed up, talking about the Isle, she changed. It was like she was ready to leave us behind. And…nothing’s the same anymore.”

The snowfall obscured Elisa’s face. She also wrapped her arms around herself, rubbing them to stave off the cold. She looked small, vulnerable, and childlike.

“Miria’s wants you back…please, come home.”

A profound weariness fell upon Jade’s shoulders. She clenched her fists and dug her fingernails deep into her numb palms, her side still searing with pain.

“All right,” she said, closing her eyes.

They attached two cables from either end of Elisa’s pod and secured them to the centipede. Jade slipped into the back of the bull and they made their way back to the farm in silence as the gold and orange light of dawn rose from the horizon.

***

Elisa and Jade arrived back at the cottage mid-morning. Gila, Tarin, Avi, and Dan sat the kitchen table with blankets draped across their shoulders, having blinked away their minds' calls for sleep.

Gila's head shot up when she noticed the girls standing in the doorway. She rose to her feet and marched toward Jade and Elisa. She pointed her walking stick directly at Jade's chest with a slightly shaky grip. She opened her mouth, yet no words came. Pounding her stick on the wooden floor with a resounding thud, Gila met Jade's gaze, her eyes ablaze with rage. "Welcome home!"

"I'm sorry," said Jade.

"Never…do…that…again!" Gila punctuated each word with a jab of her stick near Jade's chest. The old woman turned and made her way to her chair beside Tarin, collapsing into it with a drawn-out sigh.

Before she could say anything else, Avi jumped from his seat and tackled Jade, holding her in a tight hug. "I thought you'd left forever," the boy admitted, on the verge of tears. Jade patted the boy on the head with a small smile.

"We all did," Tarin said flatly.

Dan sat hunched over in a kitchen chair, his features drawn. "Why?" was all he said.

"I thought it would be better if I left this family alone now," Jade said as she gently brushed Avi aside.

"But you are family now," said Dan.

Jade flinched, and not only from the burn in her side.

"You did more than I could."

"Dan," Jade muttered. He stepped forward and took her in a tight embrace.

"I'll be in the workshop," he said as he parted from Jade. He ran upstairs to retrieve his coat before leaving, closing the front door with a soft click.

Everyone remained in place, as if afraid to move.

"Could I see Miria?" Jade whispered.

Gila nodded.

"Of course," said Tarin, avoiding her gaze. "But none of this is your fault. Understood?"

Jade shuffled outside Miria's room, took a breath, and rapped on the door. "It's me."

"Of course, it is," a hoarse voice replied.

Jade cringed at the frailty in her voice. She twisted the door handle and crept inside. Miria lay in bed, illuminated by soft candlelight, her thickly bandaged arm wrapped in a sling. Jade sank into the chair beside her bed.

"I don't know what to say," said Jade, clinging to the chair, struggling to meet her friend's weary gaze.

"I do. Thank you," Miria rasped, her eyes closed.

Jade stared into the distance. She leaned back in her chair, head bobbing and yawning until sleep overwhelmed her. Miria's gaze rested on Jade before closing her own eyes and dozing off into a light sleep.

Jade woke to the cranking of gears in the work shed, squinting over her shoulder through the window. Below, the workday continued with Elisa collecting eggs and Avi trailing behind with a basket. If not for their drawn faces and empty eyes, the scene would seem like any other day on the farm.

Miria was awake, sitting upright and gazing down at her injured arm. It seemed she had been in that position for a while.

"You should get some more rest," said Jade.

She turned to face her. Her eyes blazed with unflinching resolve. "I'm coming with you to the Isle."

Jade jumped back a little in her seat. She pressed her hands to Miria's shoulders, urging her to lie down. "I…you don't know what you're saying."

"I know exactly what I'm saying!" she said, prying Jade's hands from her shoulders. "Do you think I can just sit here after that? That creature wasn't like anything I've ever seen before. Something is very wrong here." "That's why I ran away," said Jade.

"What do you mean?"

"Roland was looking for an excuse to banish him, if the dragon didn't kill us first. A monstrous dragon just like that attacked my home, and then another one comes here to attack us. Of course it did" she said with a low, sardonic chuckle. "Each night after I ran away, I dreamed about a future, back home, with my father, and Grant, where everything was back to normal. I still think about that future. How sad is that?"

"They've turned all our lives upside down," said Miria.

"Whatever they're doing on the Isle, maybe it's twisting the whole world around."

"If that's true, then you shouldn't go there without me. It would be too dangerous. We'll find the answers together," Miria said.

"What about your family?" Jade sat up with a start. "I can handle this on my own!"

"They're why I have to go!" Miria snapped, rising slightly before falling back onto the bed, gazing blankly up at the ceiling. "The world's falling apart around us., and I can't pretend it's not happening. It isn't what they would do." She grasped her stone with her good hand.

"They'll keep looking for your stone," said Jade.

Miria's eyes were fixed into a determined glare.

Jade sighed. "Neither of us is in any shape to go anywhere for a long time. Besides, the Isle…it seems farther away than ever," she said.

"We can do it. It's just going to take some…unconventional methods. That's why you'll need me. I'm probably one of the few people in the world who could pull this off," said Miria.

"At least your modesty is still intact," Jade giggled lightly.

"I mean it. It's the birthplace of magic. That's why we need a creature that's from there to take us across the waters and not a ship," Miria continued.

"You're not suggesting what I think you are?"

"We need a dragon," confirmed Miria.

Jade gaped in shock and confusion. "I…are, are you all right? I think you need more rest."

Miria gave a derisive snort. "It makes perfect sense! If we're going, we have to do better than my parents. We'll find a dragon to take us."

"You can't be serious! After what just happened!"

“We can’t rely on a crew with bravado but no brains for navigating a place like the Isle,” said Miria. “The normal rules don’t apply there. We need a proper guide…one from the Isle. If anyone can get us to the Isle on the back of a dragon, it’s me.” She unconsciously flexed her bandaged arm slightly, wincing from the pain. “On our own terms, right?” Miria gave Jade a weak smile. She lay back on the bed and stared up at the ceiling. “Take me with you?” Her tone edged on desperation.

Jade slumped forward, rubbing her forehead; almost wishing she could return to her lonely days on the run inside an unreliable, glitching pod. “What choice do I have?”

Chapter 10

The family's rare ventures outside became a somber occasion. The dragon corpse was a grim reminder of recent events. A quiet melancholy settled on the farm; everyone continued to go through the motions of daily farm life in a haze. Jade's thoughts lingered on her father and Grant, a sense of helplessness settling in her chest. *The list of people I've let down has grown longer since that night,* she thought.

"Don't tell the others, not yet, anyway. They have enough to worry about," said Miria during one of Jade's visits to her bedside.

Jade nodded, keeping her head down. After a while, her gaze turned to the window where a snowstorm raged outside. "What about Dan, Elisa, and Avi?" she said.

A long pause followed. "We don't need to talk about this now."

"I nearly abandoned them! Now I'm whisking their sister away to ride off to a cursed island on a dragon!"

"You make it sound like a kidnapping," said Miria with a low, rasping chuckle.

"I'm tired of secrets and lies."

Miria sighed. "All right, but only the kids. Gran and Pa aren't ready for this yet."

"This feels wrong," said Jade.

"I should rephrase; I'm not ready for them to hear our plans," said Miria. "Are you?"

She thought back to the night she returned after running away. "No, no, I'm not."

Dan, Elisa, and Avi filed into Jade's room. Jade peered over the banister, ensuring that Tarin and Gila were still in the kitchen. She dashed into her room, softly clicking the door shut behind her.

"Have a seat. I need to tell you something," she said in a hushed whisper.

"Why are you whispering? And why are we all crammed in this dusty old room?" Elisa said.

“I don’t feel as though I should be in a lady’s room,” Dan said, his gaze uneasily flitting about the room. “Is there anywhere else we could have this conversation?”

“Surely you’ve been in your sisters” rooms before?” said Jade, gawking at Dan in disbelief.

“Not since Miria and me were little. She threatened to set a dozen dragons on me if I set foot in there. She didn’t have any, of course. But I didn’t know that at the time!”

Elisa and Avi shared a bemused look before breaking into giggles.

“Shhh!” Jade held a finger to her mouth. “Miria doesn’t want your Gran and Pa finding out just yet,” she said, dropping her voice to an even lower tone, crouched down beside her bed.

“What are you talking about?” Elisa asked, lowering her voice to a whisper as well.

Jade’s grip on her knees tightened. “She wants to come with me.” Silence descended.

“That makes sense. For her.” Elisa pressed her index and forefinger to her temple and heaved a sigh.

"The more you talked about going to the Isle, the more she wanted to go, too. It's not that surprising," Dan observed.

"Miria is leaving?" Avi nearly rose from his seat.

"I tried to talk her out of it," said Jade. "I'm sorry."

Avi averted his gaze, saying nothing.

"Miria's at her most vulnerable now. Of course, she'd want something to cling to. And she has a chance to complete our parents' work. It'd be like a lifeline to her," Dan muttered.

"But what about…everything?" said Jade.

Elisa sighed. "Once Miria's decided something, it would be easier to teach a dragon to dance than talk her out of it," she said.

"Speaking of doing impossible things with dragons…," Jade trailed off.

The siblings fixed her with an expectant look. She shrank under their gazes. "Miria wants to ride one to the Isle," she blurted out.

They gaped in open-mouthed silence. "Has she lost her mind?" Elisa said at last.

"That was my reaction," said Jade with a sigh. Elisa shot up from the bed, flung open Jade's door, and marched down the hall.

"Elisa? What are you doing?" Jade's voice rose as she chased after the younger girl.

"Are you all right up there, girls?" Tarin yelled from the kitchen.

"Uh, fine. Thanks," said Jade.

She tried to shuffle in front of the younger girl to block her path to Miria's room, but Elisa brushed her back.

"Get out of the way," said Elisa and strode into her sister's room with a steadfast determination blazing in her eyes. She waited for Jade to follow before closing the door behind her with a soft click.

"What are you doing?" Elisa demanded, standing by her sister's bed, arms crossed.

Miria pushed herself up. "I was resting like I'm supposed to until you all came barging in."

“It didn’t go well,” Jade said, creeping out from behind Elisa and offering Miria an apologetic look. Dan lurched the door open, peering from behind it and throwing the girls a questioning look.

“You might as well come in if you’re going to loiter in the doorway,” said Miria.

He slunk inside with Avi shuffling in behind him.

“Can I ask what you’re all doing in here?” Miria said, pushing herself into a sitting position.

“Wondering if you have a death wish.” Elisa stared long and hard at her sister, with a fury that Jade hadn’t seen since that night in the forest.

“I knew this was a bad idea,” Miria muttered under her breath. “Okay.” She raised her voice. “Everyone, come back later.” She clutched her forehead, immediately regretting the decision to yell. “I don’t need this.”

“Neither do we,” said Elisa.

“She has a point,” said Jade.

“Since when do you two get along?” Miria huffed.

“What’s going on up there, you lot?” Gila bellowed from the kitchen.

“Nothing!” everyone yelled in unison.

Miria held her head, taking in a deep breath. “Nothing makes sense anymore.” Her voice fell to a hushed whisper. “All I know is that I can’t sit and watch the world fall apart. I’m still here because of Jade. I’m not about to do something that will get me, or her, killed. I don’t expect you to understand, but I want you to trust me.”

“I don’t understand,” Dan said as he ran a hand through his messy brown hair. “But I know when you’ve fixed your mind on something, that’s the end of the matter.

Miria laid back in bed with a grunt. She turned to Avi, who was peering from behind Dan, appearing lost and confused.

“It will be okay,” said Miria.

“You always say that,” said the boy. He sighed and shuffled from the room without a word.

***

Miria rarely left her room. Gila would slip in to offer her food while Jade, Avi, and Elisa snuck in to see her at random intervals, which she would grumble about. She allowed them to stay so long as they made "precious little noise." Avi would perch on the side of her bed, neither saying a word. Afterward, he'd either help Dan in the work shed or Elisa with collecting firewood and tending to the chickens. Jade asked him for help with magic to cheer him up, but he just shook his head and helped around the farm instead.

The vacant chair between Avi and Jade during mealtimes remained a solemn reminder of her absence. Miria announced her presence with a groan one morning as she fumbled down the stairs. Both Dan and Jade moved quickly to her side.

Miria waved them away and they returned to the table as she took her seat, exchanging a halfhearted grin through her unkempt hair.

"Miria?" Avi said, regarding her with confused interest.

"I'm still here, kid," she said, patting the boy's head absently.

"Hello, stranger," said Tarin. "It's been a long time." He rose from his chair and searched the cupboards for cutlery and a plate. He placed them in front of her with an enormous grin that stayed in place as he made his way back to his seat, pointing to her with unabashed joy.

"Thought I should rejoin the outside world," said Miria, sprinkling fruit onto her plate.

A quiet chatter rippled across the table, with awkward, tentative laughter.

"You seem like yourself again, girl," Gila observed.

"I'm starting to feel that way," she said and took in a breath before continuing. "I think I know what would help even more."

Dan ate his porridge faster, coughing a little. Jade picked at her porridge, keeping her head down. Meanwhile, both Elisa and Avi sat up straighter, keeping their heads down.

Tarin and Gila observed the room with a suspicious eye. "What did you have in mind?" Tarin asked.

"Some fresh air," Miria said with a shrug. "I'd like to see the forests and valleys again. It feels like so long since I've seen the outside world."

"I…I think it's an excellent idea," said Jade.

"If she wants to go out. I'll go with her, and so will Jade," said Dan.

"Well, you can't stay inside forever," Gila agreed. "Just as long as Jade and Dan go along with you."

"Of course, I wouldn't go anywhere without my new babysitters," Miria said drolly.

"Now, Miria, it's not like that and you know it," Tarin said with a sigh.

"Isn't it?" she said, shoveling her food at a faster pace.

"You should say something," Avi grabbed his elder sister's sleeve, forcing her to stop eating.

"Let me eat. I've said everything that I need to, Avi." Jade and Miria exchanged nervous expressions.

"I sincerely hope that you have," Gila added with raised eyebrows, peering at her granddaughter as she raised a cup of tea to her lips.

Chapter 11

Jade, Miria, and Dan's search began during the autumn months soon after their injuries began to recover. However, a thick sheet of snow still stubbornly clung to Vansh. The mechanical bull plodded through the snow with dogged determination until it pulled into a deserted valley. They left the bull by an old oak tree and made their way through the Eastern Valley.

"There should be ice dragons in this territory," said Miria. "These dragons don't breathe fire. They have an easygoing temperament too, at least more than most breeds."

"Still, a flying pod that looks like a dragon would be more reliable than an actual, fire-breathing dragon," said Dan.

"The best way to get to an unpredictable land of magic is with an unpredictable, magic creature," said Miria. She leaped over a log and winced, brushing away Jade's hands on her shoulders. 'I'm still quite capable, thank you."

While a dull pain still stung Jade's sides, she moved throughout the forest with more ease than her friend.

"Look," said Dan, pointing to a set of gigantic claw prints in the snow.

A deep, rumbling growl coursed through the earth, causing it to shake lightly. The three exchanged knowing glances.

"Maybe we should rest a little before meeting our new friend." Dan looked to the horizon.

"I think we should get it out of the way, but resting is a good idea, too," Miria admitted. "We should prepare." She absently rubbed at the leather glove she wore over her burned hand. "Mentally and physically."

Jade's gaze wandered in the direction of the dragon's roars. She took in a deep breath.

"What do you think, Jade?" said Miria, snapping her from her thoughts.

"Hmm? Oh, good idea," she said as her gaze fell on her friend's gloved hand.

Dan did the heavy lifting, while the girls unpacked and did the smaller tasks. After setting up their tents, Jade shuffled in beside Miria, and they both gazed up without exchanging a word. Jade fidgeted, waiting until Miria's chest slowly began to rise and fall with the rhythm of sleep. Her gaze lingered on her a moment before she slipped from the tent and stood before Dan's, where he was covered in blankets and softly snoring.

She took slow, gingerly steps away from the campsite.

When Dan stirred in his sleep, Jade jumped, leaping over backward and crossing her arms. She a ball of blue light engulfed her before fading away, leaving her still standing in place.

"What are you doing?" asked Miria.

Jade ignored her. She closed her eyes and took a deep crossing her arms once more. She vanished in a spark of light and reappeared in the clearing where they heard the dragon. She stood at the edge of a steep hill. A huge mound covered in a thick layer of snow lay at the bottom; the sound of its steady breathing and the long silvery tail flickering about were the only signs of life.

Jade breathed deeply to steady her shaking and held her palms upward, summoning a blue ball of light in her hands. A large yellow eye snapped open, peeking through the snow. She shrank back as the beast shook off the snow and unfurled its body, revealing a long neck lined with silvery scales and white horns that twisted up in two sharp spikes. It had a protruding snout with nostrils that shot out streams of smoke.

It looked down at the newcomer, silent and still, slightly cocking its head to the side. Jade stayed fixed in place.

"Easy now," she whispered. "I need your help." She held up the light, hoping it would react. It continued to gaze down at her, unmoving.

Footsteps approached. Miria and Dan stood at the top of the hill, breathless and watching in horror. The dragon approached the light, its movements slow and uncertain. Miria slid down the hillside, stumbling toward Jade and the dragon. She stole a disapproving glance at her companion in-between ragged breaths. Dan joined them, standing close behind, his arms wrapped around the two of them. The dragon's amber eyes widened, and it lowered its head to the light, enchanted by the stone's glow.

Miria let the pendant fall around her neck, shakily reaching out with her good hand to touch the dragon's twisted horn. The creature lowered its body, resting on the ground and regarding the trio with a mixture of curiosity and abject confusion. After a while, the dragon soon curled back into a ball with a grumble and settled back to sleep. Miria gestured for them to leave, turning her back to Jade. They walked back to the campsite in silence.

"I was trying to help," whispered Jade.

"Miria paused before pivoting on her heel. "Maybe you should have invited the expert on dragons? This works on normal dragons," Miria held up her stone pendant. "It's going to get us to the Isle. I'll do what my parents couldn't."

Jade's gaze fell to the barren trees.

"I thought…," Miria said, stepping toward Jade, a fire burning in her eyes. "You know what? It doesn't even matter what I think. You've made that much clear."

"You know I had to!" Jade said. "After what happened that night."

"You can't do this by yourself!"

"Well, maybe I should!" Jade shouted, surprising herself and Miria with the ferocity of her tone.

"If that's how you feel," Miria said.

Dan dashed forward to catch up with his sister, throwing her a disapproving look as he passed her. Jade shook her head, running a palm over her face, and trudged behind the pair. They packed up camp in silence and trudged to the bull.

Dan helped Jade inside, throwing her a look of exasperation. He shook his head and said, "Jumping in front of a dragon doesn't solve all of life's problems, you know."

"I'll come up with a better strategy next time," she muttered before shuffling into the metal giant. "Thanks for the advice, though." She managed a weak smile.

Dan turned to his sister, who waited outside. Dan took her hand, gingerly helping Miria inside the pod.

“At least we’re all safe and alive, and we can tell everyone all about our new friend,” Dan said.

“What a joy that will be,” Miria said flatly.

“It’s a shame we can’t take him home; Avi would love him.” Dan rested a hand on the top of the hatch.

“Dan, we both know what a terrible idea bringing an eight-foot dragon to the village would be,” Miria pointed out. “For multiple reasons.”

“It’d be safer than telling Gran and Pa what we’ve actually been up to.”

“Maybe we should just get it over with,” Jade mumbled, glancing behind her.

“We will,” said Miria.” But we need to make more progress with the dragon first.”

“I hate to keep things from them, especially something this big,” Dan said as he tapped his fingers on the rim of the hatch. Snowflakes fell around them. “Besides, they’re already suspicious,” he said. “And it won’t take much for them to get it out of Avi. Jade’s right; might as well tell ’em now and get it over with.”

Miria sighed. “Unfortunately, you both have a point. But I’ll do the talking, okay?”

Dan threw his sister a nervous grin before snapping the bull’s hatch closed.

Chapter 12

“You are all out of your minds if you think you’re going on a joyride to that death trap of an island on a flying death trap!” Gila shouted, pacing up and down the kitchen before taking a seat next to Tarin.

“That went better than I thought,” Dan whispered to Miria from the side of his mouth.

Tarin smoked his pipe while he stared into the distance, still unable to form words. Jade and Dan shifted about uncomfortably in their seats. Elisa sat beside Miria, hands folded, her expression unreadable.

Dan suggested that Avi go to the work shed to start on a project they had planned together. The three agreed that he should not have to see the fallout from their secret activities.

“I know what I’m doing,” said Miria, meeting her grandmother’s glare with an equally fierce one.

“That’s what your father told me,” Gila said. “If you have to go ahead with this madness, I’d prefer you to gather a crew to take you. Take your time and plan this properly.”

"We stand a better chance of getting into the home of dragons with a dragon. Rather than a ship and a group of people who don't even know what they're doing," Miria insisted.

"But how would you get back?" Tarin finally found his voice.

"The same way we get there. I can either call on the dragon that takes us or just find another. It's not like they'll be a shortage of them."

"And how far do you think you'll get in your condition?" said Gila, leaning forward slightly. The hand on her walking stick quivered. "This might seem like some grand adventure to you, but you don't know the risks!"

"I don't know the risks?" Miria slapped her hands onto the table, causing her to wince. "The world's falling apart. We all know it. But I'm choosing not to wait until there's nothing but ash to wonder how it happened."

"I've heard all the big ideas about saving the world before. Heroic ideals got your parents killed," said Gila.

"I won't let anything happen…again," said Jade, rising from her seat. She winced and held her side. She shook off the pain and took in a raspy breath. Gila and Tarin's heads rose, the young woman's steely gaze commanding their attention. "I promise."

Jade crossed her arms, then pressed her fingers onto the surface of the table.

"What are you doing?" Gila asked.

"You're a good teacher." A soft tremble began to ripple through the house and gold coins flowed from Jade's palms, rapidly piling up on the table "This is all the money from my father's treasure trove back home. Use it to rebuild the work shed, expand the farm—anything. Just know this is a token of my promise to return from the Isle with your granddaughter in one piece."

"You forgot to mention that's a promise by Jade of House Sol," Miria said, her shoulders shaking with her soft chuckles.

Jade's solemn resolve broke, and she dissolved into laughter as well. "You're right. That's unforgivable!" She slammed a fist on the table.

"I am very confused," Elisa admitted.

Miria shook her head. "Don't mind me," she said.

"We already told you that we don't want your money," said Tarin.

"Have you ever considered that this is what we all need?" asked Dan.

"What are you talking about, Daniel?" said Gila.

"We can't expect either of them to stay. None of us want Jade to go alone, and if anyone can make it to the Isle, it's Miria. And I'm not letting them out of my sight, even if all I can do is watch." He heaved a sigh, shoulders sagging.

"Dan, you're still needed here on the farm. Now more than ever," said Tarin.

"You don't have to do this," said Jade.

"I couldn't help Rosh or Miria, but maybe I can be of some use now."

Tarin exchanged a tired look with Gila. "They're too much like their parents."

"You don't need to remind me," she said, rubbing her temple with a sigh. "It was only a matter of time until you ran off." A slight tremble in her hand loosened her grip on her walking stick.

Tarin sighed, about to rise from his seat to fetch a drink of water when Elisa finished washing the dishes and took a seat at the end of the table. "You should trust them. They'll look out for each other," she said. Miria shot her a perplexed look and she shrugged in reply, offering them a half-smile. "I trust Jade."

"You should be more worried about her," Dan said, gesturing with his thumb to Elisa.

"Oh, shut up, Dan!" she said. She turned to their grandparents. "Look, I'm scared, too. But if Miria thinks it's a good idea, then I'll trust her, and I think you should too."

Gila closed her eyes. "You lot will be the death of us."

"Well, we can't exactly tie them down," Tarin said regretfully. He leaned forward, and his gaze held an intensity and conviction that demanded attention. "You need to come back. All of you." He inclined his head to Jade.

"Come back? Dan, what's happening?" a small voice asked from the doorway. A snow-covered Avi trudged into the kitchen, leaving a trail of mud and ice throughout the house. He stood ragged-breathed, hazel eyes searching for answers.

"Av! Take your boots off and sit down." Dan approached his younger brother, squatting down and resting his broad hands on the boy's shoulders. "We need to talk."

***

"You packed the sandwiches and drawing gear, right, Jade?" Dan shouted over his shoulder as the bull chugged toward the now familiar destination.

She rested a hand on the knapsack and said, "Tarin and Gila wouldn't let me leave without it. And now we'll have a way to show Avi and the others the dragon."

"We can't tame this dragon if you treat our outings like a picnic," Miria mumbled from the back of the pod. She dug her fingernails into Jade's shoulders.

"Miria," Jade whispered, throwing her gaze over her shoulder at Miria.

"Uh, oh right," said Miria. She promptly loosened her grip on Jade's shoulders, her cheeks burning.

"There's nothing to worry about now that we have the dragon expert with us," Jade yelled so she could be heard over the rattling engine.

The bull pulled into the forest with a lurch, jerking them forward somewhat.

"That's always the worst part," Miria complained. The side hatch creaked open, and they descended the ramp. The three began their trek into the hills, slinking around the barren trees until they reached the hill where the dragon lay below. It was in a large crater where it spent its days snoozing, curled into a ball, the silvery scales peeking through the sheet of snow that blanketed the large beast.

The three of them sat perched at the top of the hill in clear view of the dragon when it woke, getting it accustomed to their presence. The dragon stretched its massive body and regarded its visitors with vague disinterest.

Miria held up the stone in front of it until it snorted in a disgruntled manner and turned away. "It's almost like a cat," she observed.

The dragon wound its body around a thick redwood, eying a meaty eagle perched on a tree . It snapped its jaws around the thin branch, crunching it into brittle pieces as the eagle glided away just in time.

"An eight-foot cat with scales and extremely sharp teeth," Miria added.

"I still wish we were going in a mechanical one," Dan grumbled.

"I just want to observe and draw," said Jade. She busied herself with drawing rough sketches of the dragon. While her talents were underdeveloped and the dragon on the page did not reflect the many shades and contours of her model, the rhythm and meditative nature of her pencil scribbling across paper had a calming effect that kept her rooted and focused.

“Jade?” said Miria.

“What is it?” Jade responded, placing her drawing utensils aside and locking eyes with her friend.

“Do…do you think I could look at your sketches?” Still refusing to make eye contact, Miria held out her hand, waiting for the drawings.

Jade shuffled closer to the other young woman, slipping the papers into her good hand with a nervous laugh. “I still need more practice. Dragons aren’t the easiest things to sketch, but I promised to show him to Avi and Elisa.” She pointed a pencil toward the snoring ice dragon.

Jade shifted about as the uneasy silence dragged on, raking her fingers through her ponytail.

Miria sifted through the papers with a keen eye and a series of low hums.

“What does that mean?” Jade inched a little closer, studying Miria’s features with nervous curiosity. After shuffling through the papers, Miria handed them to Dan, who also inspected them.

Miria chuckled before promptly regaining her composure and cleared her throat. "It means that you have talent. I think you have a great eye for detail and should keep practicing."

Dan passed the papers to Miria, who returned them to Jade.

"Uh, thank you," said Jade, peering over Miria's shoulder at Dan, who offered her a grin and a thumbs up.

Chapter 13

"We need to leave when the weather calms, as much as it can, anyway," said Miria. She turned to Gila. "I'll need one of your predictions, Gran."

The old woman nodded, gazing into the crackling fire. She told them to leave in three days, when the sun shone like a lighthouse beacon through the gray clouds, and the snowfall rested.

As the days drew nearer until the day of their journey arrived, Jade practiced her magic. On their second to last day, a persistent knocking interrupted her attempts to teleport herself from the floor to her bed. She dusted herself off with a sigh, rose to her feet, and approached the door.

"Yes?" She creaked the door open and peered around the corner. Incessant knocking often meant unexpected tackle hugs from Avi. "That knocking was a little too enthusiastic," said Jade. "What are you planning?" Dan, Avi, and Elisa waited outside for her with eager smiles.

"You worry too much," said Elisa.

"That's concerning coming from you," Jade scoffed.

"Look, we came here to give you a surprise, okay?" Elisa pulled Jade from the doorway by the hand.

"Come on. Follow us!" Dan raced down the stairs, barely containing his excitement. The three led her down the stairs and outside to the work shed.

"Are you going to show me saddles for the dragon?" Jade asked.

"Even better!" Dan pushed open the work shed door and rushed to where the centipede rested. He pulled off the tarp covering the machine and waved to the centipede with a grand gesture.

"You changed it!" said Jade.

"You won't have any problems with it now," said Dan. The centipede was finely polished and had fewer legs that were replaced by four sturdy rounded ones with longer, claw-like limbs that dug into the wooden floorboards of the work shed. "Your original pod wasn't meant for long-distance travel across country."

"It looks more like a chimera now," observed Jade, running a hand over one of its elongated legs.

"It kind of does now that you mention it," said Elisa. "A horrifying creature from the other realm, never allowed to enter our world."

Avi snickered in agreement.

"Funny," Dan said in a flat tone.

"We're sorry," Jade said with a smile. "Please continue."

Dan nodded. "I made some changes to make it durable in case you ever need it again. I used the parts the Mechanic gave me and came up with the design myself. I guess should have discussed it with you first. Hope you don't mind."

"Of course, I don't! The Mechanic would be proud, and the others would love it. You'll get some good use out of it."

"What do you mean?" Dan asked.

"I'd thought about selling it, but there's no need now that we're going by dragon," said Jade. In fact, I probably won't be needing it after the journey. Dad and I will find another pod, so I thought I'd give it to you. Consider it a present."

Dan's mouth fell open. "Are you sure?"

"It can stay here as a symbol of our promise." Jade turned to Elisa and Avi. "The centipede will wait here until we come home, and Dan can take you to the markets in it."

Avi avoided her gaze, shuffling his feet while mumbling in a barely audible voice, “How ’bout now?”

“You want to take her for a ride now, Avi?” Dan approached Avi, squatting, so he was at eye level with his younger brother. His eyes shone with childlike glee, and he bounced slightly.

“Is that a good idea?” Elisa asked. “Even with the invisibility setting back, it would still be a big, unnecessary risk. If the wrong people see the pod, it will put Jade in danger.”

“Yeah, you’re right. I’m sorry, Jade,” said Avi. He scuffed his feet on the wooden floorboards and shuffled out of the shed.

“No, let’s go. It will only be for a short time,” said Jade.

Dan, Jade, and Avi crammed into the tight space of the pod. Dan sat in the front seat, eagerly tapping the buttons on the board and pulling the lever that made the pod roar to life. Jade gripped Avi’s slim shoulders as he squirmed into place behind Dan.

“The centipede looked way bigger on the outside.”

“She can still move just as good, Avi. Just wait and see,” Dan said, switching on stealth mode. Elisa waved goodbye to the now invisible mechanical beast that crept into the shrubbery.

"It's like the bull, only smoother," Avi marveled, gripping Dan's shoulders tighter as the metal centipede crawled over a log and weaved around the snow-laden willows.

"You know how much I love that pod, but I have to agree," said Dan.

The mechanical creature bounded across the forest with ease. He pulled a lever, and the centipede crouched down, its legs contracting before digging its forelegs into a willow tree and beginning to climb it. The tree lightly trembled during the ascent, with snow falling over the pod's portholes before revealing a view of the forest floor, the machine twisting around the tree with ease.

It wound higher up the tree before its head lulled back, its claws still embedded in the tree. The pod slipped downward slightly, the creature's claws ripping along the tree bark. The three fell back a little, clinging to whoever or whatever they could to stay in place. A loud, insistent hooting was followed by a persistent pecking and scratching at the outside of the pod.

"Dan, what's happening? How can they see us?" Avi leaned against his brother, wrapping his arms around his older brother's neck.

"I don't know Avi, but you'll have to let go," Dan yelled. "I'll take us down now, I promise." He patted Avi's arm before slowly maneuvering the centipede backward.

"Okay," he whispered, untangling himself from his brother.

Jade leaned into a porthole. A brood of giant owls hovered over the pod. Their cobalt blue eyes bored into her. The relentless pecking and scratching grew louder. Jade shoved the porthole open. However, she could not see past the mass of feathers and claws that dove at her. She jumped back, slamming the porthole shut.

"Dan, get us down now! These things are possessed!"

"I'm trying!" He began pulling levers and pressing buttons in quick succession.

The metal beast's claws scratched against the willow bark as it slipped from the tree. The owls ripped a foreleg off of the pod. Jade and Avi fell to the back, while Dan barely maintained his grip on the controls.

"You two okay?" Dan yelled over his shoulder.

"These birds are already helping us down," said Jade. She rubbed her side and carefully moved Avi off of her while checking that he was uninjured. She closed her eyes, practicing the breathing exercises Gila taught her. She crossed her arms with open palms before closing them again. “Avi, I want you to get ready to send a puff of magic out of the porthole.”

“Okay.” The boy nodded and prepared his magic.

“Jade, are you sure?” Dan asked.

“It’s okay, Dan. She knows what’s she’s doing.

“I know, kid.” Dan smiled thinly.

Both Jade and Avi scrambled to the portholes, thrusting them open and releasing a burst of pale blue magic from their palms. The owls shrieked and dispersed around the forest. As they released their talons from the shaking tree, Dan lowered the pod in gradual steps. The newly installed legs that remained shuffled backward to the ground. The upper half of the machine leaned against the willow, while the lower half was on the ground.

“I’ll try to keep her steady,” Dan said.

The owls hovered over them, talons preparing to dive on the machine once more.

“We’ll need something bigger than that to scare them off.” Jade opened the top hatch, preparing to push herself upward onto the hull. “Those certainly aren’t your usual owls, so I’ll handle this, okay?”

"But there are so many of them," Avi protested, tugging on Jade's robes.

"I can't let you risk yourself," she said, pulling away from the boy.

"But why is it okay for you to put yourself at risk?"

"Avi," Jade muttered in surprise. She perched herself on the hull. She extended a hand to the boy.

He took Jade's outstretched hand, sitting on the opposite side of the hull.

The owls circled around them with increasing speed.

"Why are they doing this? What's wrong with them?" Avi asked.

"Just get ready. Looks like they're coming to tear the pod, and us, to shreds."

The owls flapped their wings in wild, erratic motions, diving toward them, talons bared, and ready to descend upon their prey with a blood-curdling screech. Jade and Avi screamed.

Jade shut her eyes and threw her hands over her head after crossing them. She held her breath.

"Jade," Avi whispered.

When she opened her eyes, a shining blue shield appeared above them. The owls continued to screech as they uselessly clawed against the magic shield.

Suddenly, they backed away, disappearing in a burst of blue light, with only the owl at the head of the brood remaining. It became smaller, shrinking down to the size of a normal owl; it glided above the trees, flying away from the damaged pod.

The other owls also diminished in size, following the owl into the sky.

Jade and Avi gripped the sides of the hull tightly as the shaky metal beast eased to the forest floor.

“That was exciting,” Dan said with a huff, mussing his messy brown hair back.

Jade approached the pod’s disembodied foreleg, running a hand over the talon marks. “And you put so much work into modifying it. I’m sorry, Dan.”

“I’m the one who should apologize,” said Dan. He rubbed the stiffness from the back of his neck after a prolonged time cramped in the pod. “I shouldn’t have taken you out on a ride. Not so soon before we’re meant to leave.”

“I don’t want you to go.” Avi turned his gaze away from them.

"You know," said Jade, crouching down beside the boy. "When my father left, I was so scared." The boy turned to her. "But you have many people around you, and we're coming back, okay?"

"I'm sorry," he mumbled.

"Hey, you have nothing to be sorry about, okay?" Dan clapped a hand on the boy's shoulder with a crooked smile.

"The others must be worried. We should head back…somehow," Jade said, turning to the disheveled pod.

"I might have an idea how we might do that, but I'll need both of you to help." Dan rolled up his sleeves and retrieved the torn-off leg, putting it back in place. "Don't have the time or tools to repair her here, so we'll need a temporary fix," he huffed.

"Oh, I know," said Jade. She knelt into the cold white earth, crossing her arms before spreading her hands. Balls made from magic spread from her hands and fused the upper leg back on the pod's body. Avi scrambled to her side and also helped to meld the leg onto the metal beast. After its legs were back in place, the three crept back inside the machine, and the mechanical centipede limped back to the cottage.

***

Elisa and Miria hurried to the scratched and battered machine as it collapsed in front of the work shed.

Dan cracked upon the pod's mouth. "We're back," he said with a lopsided grin and an oil-smeared face. Jade and Avi popped up from the hatch, their hair disheveled and their clothes soaked.

"Did you fight in a battle?" Miria rushed to the side of the pod, extending her uninjured arm to Avi, helping him climb down from the machine.

"You could say that." Jade hopped from the pod and went to the front of the machine as Dan slithered from the pod's mouth.

Elisa bobbed up and down to inspect the pod's damage. "What are all these scratches from?"

"Giant killer owls," Jade said with a shrug.

"What?" said Miria and Elisa in unison.

"We'll explain inside," Dan said, inspecting his soaking clothes.

"It had better be a good explanation. Gran and Pa are putting on preparations for tonight." Elisa gestured for the three to come inside.

Miria walked beside Jade. “This sounds like an adventure that I’m glad I missed out on,” she said.

“At least you’ll get to be around for the next one,” said Jade.

“Uh, I hope,” Miria retorted as Elisa opened the cottage door.

Gila and Tarin breathed a sigh of relief when they entered the cottage. “You already look like you’ve traveled halfway across the world,” Tarin said as he gestured to their disheveled state.

“Never a dull moment with this lot,” Gila said, shaking her head in exasperated amusement.

“It was my fault,” said Avi, shuffling forward. “They wanted to take me for a ride in Jade’s pod to cheer me up, and we ran into all these weird owls who could see us! And we even managed—”

“Owls? Owls, you say?” Gila rose from her seat. “Were there many?” she asked, inching forward and crouching down slightly to be at eye level with the boy.

“More owls than I’ve ever seen!”

“Were they big? And did they have pale blue eyes?”

Avi, Dan, and Jade nodded.

“We scared them off, and they turned into one owl when they left, but there was something very…” Jade searched for a fitting term, “off about them!”

“Off indeed.” Gila began pacing up and down, tapping her walking stick on the dining room floor. “This is a bad omen,” she muttered to herself.

“You’ve seen them before?” Dan asked.

“Unfortunately, I have. You’re lucky that’s all the wily old troublemaker did,” Gila said, shaking her head.

“What do you mean? Was that some kind of shapeshifter?” asked Jade, regarding the older woman with a bewildered expression.

“We call them shapeshifters, but they’re chaos spirits,” said Gila. “There aren’t many of them around, not that I know of, at least.”

“Didn’t one give that stone to your family?” said Jade.

Gila ceased her pacing and rubbed her temples, groaning in frustration. “The three of you had best clean yourselves up. The rest of you can help prepare dinner.”

Dan, Avi, and Jade changed their clothes and cleaned themselves before joining the family in the dining room. A large roast chicken, surrounded by corn, peas, and potatoes, awaited them.

"Thanks to Jade, we can now afford to eat well without relying on the food we gathered before this never-ending snow set in," Tarin said, scooping up a spoonful of vegetables.

Jade offered him a slight smile while busily piling the food onto a plate, intending to eat as much as possible. She chuckled as Avi tried to snatch up Gila's glass of wine, only for her to bat his hand away. Every time Jade gazed around the table, she reminded herself that this was the last time she would have a meal at the Atkins home for a long time, perhaps forever.

Miria slinked up to her room as Dan opened his violin case. "Not staying for the celebrations?" Tarin asked.

"I told you, rest is more important than this," Miria said as she waved to Dan's violin case.

"We all need this," explained Tarin. "And we thought it might be good for you. It's still early. Would you stay a little longer?"

"Thanks, but all I need is rest," said Miria. She bid everyone good night before trudging up the steps.

After the final dance, Avi and Elisa dragged Jade from the kitchen by the arm and into the next room.

"Dan, I may need to call for help later!" she cried out.

"I'll be right here," he said with a casual wave, sitting back in his chair.

"We have something for you." Elisa said, ignoring her brother. Avi dived behind the foot of the staircase and came back with a large knapsack in his arms. He handed it to Elisa, who removed a tatty sketchbook with Isle of Dragons inscribed on the front.

"Did you steal that from your sister's room?" said Jade.

Elisa held it out to her. "We want you to have this."

"Thanks, but I can't take this."

"We want you to use it for Miria's sake," said Elisa.

"What do you mean?"

"Someone has to complete this notebook," Avi said. "But she still can't write well with her left hand. She'll need help, and you have the skills to do it."

"Well, passable skills," said Elisa. She firmly pressed the sketchbook into Jade's hands. "The three of you are heading into the unknown. You've got to figure this out together somehow, right?"

"Elisa," said Jade, flicking through the empty pages with a smile. She closed her eyes and snapped the sketchbook closed. "I've been such an idiot."

"Can't argue with that," Elisa agreed with a smug grin.

"Thank you," said Jade, and the three of them dissolved into laughter.

When the celebrations were over, Jade made her way to Miria's room and knocked on the door. "It's me. I have something for you."

The door creaked open slightly, and a groggy Miria peeked at her around the door. "This had better be good," she said with a yawn.

Jade slid the notebook through the door. "Here; two small thieves stole this. Said they wanted me to help fill up the pages. Strange, I know."

She regarded the notebook with a blank stare. "Oh," she said at last with a half-smile. "I'll tell the little ratbags off tomorrow. But you can hold on to it for now," she said, pressing the door closed. Jade gazed down at the notebook with a growing smile, the realization dawning on her that Miria planned the whole thing .

Chapter 14

Even as the cold persisted, hints of change snuck through the frozen land. Seedlings sprouted, and tendrils of grass peeked through the snow. Meanwhile, animals either stayed hidden away in prolonged hibernation or wandered from their homes in a state of confusion. Farmers grew weary with the everlasting winter, not knowing when their crops would grow again. Rumors that the Vanshian economy was in a sorry state spread throughout the land.

"Hardly a surprise when we can't grow a damned thing," Gila said, occupying the rocking chair.

Dan rose as the family rooster announced a new day and headed to the work shed. He collected the blueprints of old projects from the Mechanic's workshop that were splayed on the work table into a neat pile. Dan folded the papers in half and slid them into his knapsack and inspected his old projects one last time. Miria sat erect in her bed, looking out at the work shed before reaching for her leather glove and sliding it over her injured hand, wincing at the action, the cold making her burnt flesh ache more keenly.

Soon after, Jade woke to make their final preparations for the journey ahead. She removed her clothing from the drawers and slid it into her knapsack.

Every member of the Atkins family remaining on the farm stood outside the cottage, stone-faced, dressed in thick robes, and still vigorously rubbing away the cold.

Miria and Jade marched toward them, knapsacks slung over their shoulders. Avi was the first to rush forward when the girls approached them, embracing Jade and then Miria. “Bring home a dragon egg, okay?”

“I will,” Miria said, “But I can’t promise it will taste fresh by the time I get it home. That is, if it doesn’t hatch first.”

Avi giggled, giving his sister a playful nudge.

Miria cleared her throat and straightened her posture. “Be good for Gran and Pa.”

He nodded. “Don’t get hurt again, okay?”

“With those two with me and a non-crazed dragon on our side, nothing can touch me.”

Avi took a step back, standing next to Elisa, who approached Miria next, “I’ll help keep the farm running smoothly. So, don’t worry too much,” she said.

“This won’t be like our parents, I promise. You won’t be without us for too long,” Miria said with a crooked grin, ruffling her sister’s hair.

“I trust you.” Elisa rearranged her hair with a grunt. She faced Jade with a look of mock disapproval, saying, “You take care of them, you hear?”

“You’re asking me this now?” Jade cocked her head to the side. “Sometimes, I don’t understand—” Elisa suddenly drew the young woman into a tight embrace. “And try to look after yourself for a change.”

Jade held her arms up. She looked about in blank surprise before returning the embrace. “Let’s have another feast when we get back, okay?”

“So, you want me to work for you the moment you get back? Typical nobility!” Elisa pulled away and smiled with tear-filled eyes.

Jade laughed, “I think I’m actually going to miss you!”

Gila and Tarin stepped forward and handed the young women stout packages of food wrapped in handkerchiefs.

"Be sure to ration it," Tarin warned. "And you all need to dress warmly." He grinned.

He turned to Jade, offering her a half-smile, his gaze fond and weary. "Remember, you can't take care of each other unless you take care of yourself first."

"Pa, we'll be fine," Miria said and hugged the old man, with Jade following suit.

When they parted, Gila took both of Miria's hands. "Come back to me, you understand?"

"I'm not like them in every way," said Miria. Gila nodded before hobbling to Jade and readjusting the cloak around her shoulders. "Remember everything that I taught you. Also, there are many beings from the other realm that roam our world," Gila warned. "Some are trustworthy, others not. Watch out for the owl with the blue eyes."

Jade nodded. "How do you know this being?"

"That is a long and complicated story," Gila said as she pressed a magic guide into Jade's hands.

"Thank you for this gift." The girl gave a deep bow of gratitude.

"Gift? What do you mean, a gift? This is only on loan!"

Jade rose from her bowing position, regarding her with confusion before breaking into a smile.

"I expect you to return that book to my shelf when you come to stay with us next! And hopefully, you can bring your father along for a feast when this damnable weather clears up!"

Jade embraced the woman. "It's a promise."

Dan soon emerged from the work shed carrying three large saddles with an array of harnesses stacked on top of one another.

"This'll make the journey much more comfortable," he said, presenting everyone with his finished work, grinning all the while.

Dan wrapped his arms around both of his grandparents in a tight bear hug. “Uh, Dan, please not so tight,” said Tarin.

“Oh, sorry,” he said and released them immediately. “I really don’t know my own strength.” Dan laughed nervously.

“So, don’t forget it,” Gila said with a playful wink and a jab of her walking stick.

“Thanks, Gran,” Dan chuckled. He turned his gaze to Avi, who shuffled his feet and stared down at the snow. Dan approached his younger brother, placing his hands under Avi’s armpits and heaving him into the air before swinging him about in a circle.

“Dan? What are you doing?” the boy yelled, laughing with confused joy.

“You’re wasting energy that you’ll need for the journey,” Elisa chafed, crossing her arms in disapproval.

“Oh, let them go,” Gila said, chuckling along with the two brothers.

Dan placed the boy back on the ground and ruffled his hair. “Take care of yourself, Avi. Keep working at your craft. You might even become as good as Gran.”

“You don’t have to worry about anything. I’ll look after everything,” Avi promised.

“Never doubted it.” Dan removed his cap and slapped it on the boy’s head, the front covering the entirety of his face. “You’ll grow into it,” Dan said as he ran a hand through his untamed muddy brown hair. “Jade and your big sister will be fine, okay?”

“I know,” said Avi as he flicked the brim of the hat up so he could see.

Dan approached Elisa, who stared into the distance, arms crossed and rubbing her body to lessen the chill that ran through her. He pulled her into a tight hug. “I know I don’t have to worry about you.”

“You should. Aside from Pa, I’m the only sensible person here who isn’t into weird things.”

“What was that, young lady?” Gila said with a raised eyebrow.

"I was joking, Gran."

"Don't work the new farmhands too hard when I'm gone, okay?" Dan said with a mischievous wink.

"I'm not making any promises," she said with a smirk.

Dan chuckled with a shake of his head before gathering up the saddle in his arms and hauling it over his shoulder. He joined Jade and Miria at the edge of the farmhouse. The three of them waved until the four figures standing outside the cottage grew smaller and smaller.

Dan filled the silence of their last journey into the Eastern Valley with a soft and cheerfully whistled tune. "I hope Smergo's ready for this," Dan readjusted the saddle over his shoulder.

"You named the dragon?" Miria deadpanned.

"I'm actually starting to like the thing. And you have to admit, Smergo's a strong, powerful name."

"Sometimes, I can't believe we're related." Miria rubbed her forehead.

"Oh, come off it; you remember Jangles, right?"

“Jangles?” Jade chortled.

“I have no idea what you’re talking about, Dan,” Miria huffed.

“It was the first dragon she brought home. It was a baby Tegu that decided to nest in Gran and Pa’s room. That was a fun night!”

“Not for me,” said Miria, pulling the hood of her cloak over her head.

Jade and Dan chuckled while Miria rolled her eyes. However, their chatter descended into silence as they walked deeper into the valley, and Jade’s thoughts wandered to Grant and her father. Did they think she had abandoned them?

“That’s far enough,” Miria declared as they reached a tall hilltop. She removed the stone from inside of her robes and held it up to the chilly winter air. “Come,” Miria whispered. The stone’s glow grew brighter, and a blue beam of light radiated upward. A roar sounded like a clap of thunder, and the ice dragon careened through the sky, its silvery scales gleaming among the gray clouds. It landed at the foot of the hill, bowing its head low.

Miria took slow, deliberate steps toward the beast and rested her good hand on the side of the dragon's head. She maintained steady eye contact with the dragon who stood in a quiet trance, mesmerized by the stone's light. With her gloved hand, Miria beckoned the dragon to sit. It promptly complied, snow flying upward as it set its massive body on the frozen earth.

"You'd better put that on now," Miria muttered with a nervous grin.

"Oh right," said Dan, entranced by the scene himself.

Securing the saddles and straps around the large, elongated creature was slow and delicate work. Miria mumbled words of reassurance to the ice dragon, keeping a steady gaze, and shined the now dimly lit stone in front of its large, glaring eyes. Occasionally, Dan accidentally pulled too tightly on the harness and earned a brief, irritable growl from the beast.

While Jade's injuries had mostly healed, a rare twinge of pain shot along her torso. Dan noted the way she winced when she lifted the saddles over her head and went to her side to help. When the pair finished, three rows of saddles lined the dragon's back.

"Not a bad job, I have to say," Dan said as he stood back, hands-on-hips, admiring his handiwork with a proud smile.

After Dan helped Miria and Jade to their saddles, he shuffled to the last one that was attached to the base of the beast's tail. Jade ran a hand over the soft leather of her saddle, her wide-legged stance awkward and unnatural, not like the times spent on horseback when she and Kaylen raced through Rioda's fields. The few horses on their property were far narrower and good companions once trust was established.

The ice dragon wriggled about a few times, making strapping in to the various buckles an awkward task. It took a few moments of muttered assurances for the beast's stirring to calm. Miria took a breath before peering over her shoulder at Jade and Dan. They answered the unspoken question with a curt nod.

"All right, let's go, old boy," she said as she gently pulled at the reins and held the glowing stone up to the grey sky. “Take us to where you and this stone first came from.” The stone glowed a deep blue, and a light suddenly shot from it that hurled across the sky like a shooting star.

The beast flapped its wings with a roar that shook the earth, and it rose from the ground, beating its wings harder and soaring into the chilled air. Jade leaned forward, digging her nails into the harness. She belatedly realized she had her eyes shut during their ascent, and she cracked open one eye. A massive storm cloud surrounded them.

“You doing all right?” Dan yelled from behind.

She looked over her shoulder and replied with a shaky smile. He returned the smile and clung to the saddle while looking rather off-color. In front of her, Miria lay back in her saddle and crowed with triumph.

The bleakness of the drawn-out winter was clear from above. A thick sheet of snow blanketed the surface of the country, with only rare patches of green peeking from the desolate winter landscape. They shot by the tiny world below, leaving villages and forests behind them in a white blur. The politics and strife of the world below seemed like a distant dream from up high. Jade closed her eyes, the cold winds rushing over her face. She threw her head back and let out a joyous laugh, letting herself enjoy the fleeting freedom that the moment offered.

Chapter 15

The dragon carried them to the southern region of Vansh, and they were nearing closer to Marda. While the region was still trapped in the nation's seemingly endless winter, the snowfall was less frequent, and more crops sprung from the ground—something they were careful not to take too much advantage of during their trips to the markets—with soldiers lurking through the streets. The three set up camp under the stars each night and stayed in forests so as not to draw unwanted attention. Jade and Dan ventured into the adjacent villages whenever they required more supplies. Miria remained with the dragon to ensure it stayed by them, which suited her because crowds "were never her thing." Dan used these opportunities to collect metal parts. If asking shop owners for spare parts failed, he slipped into scrapyards, putting discarded parts into an empty knapsack, and hauling it back to camp.

On a warm night, the three gathered around a campfire in the middle of a dense forest. The ice dragon curled up in a ball behind Miria, who roasted several pieces of fish on a skewer over the open flame. Dan scribbled on pieces of paper with a pencil with two small rectangular metal objects nestled on the log beside him. He'd place his sketches to the side at random intervals to browse through his tools and tinker with objects, linking wires together and screwing parts in place.

"When will we find out the details of your project, Dan?" Miria asked. "Those strange sounds coming from it are making me curious."

"That's a secret," Dan mumbled, screwing a gear into place. "Just a small project I'm taking from mind to the drawing board, you could say."

"I hope we get to see the big reveal of your little contraptions sooner rather than later," said Miria.

"Don't worry. They'll be ready to go soon," said Dan.

"Then I look forward to it," Miria said with a shrug.

"I'm here if you ever need any help with your invention," said Jade, looking up from her book. She sat with her legs crossed and Gila's magic guide nestled on her lap. At times while studying the manual, she placed it on the ground to cross her arms and throw a burst of blue magic from her arms. She muttered the word horse repeatedly, crossing her arms and releasing them and concentrating the blue energy that emerged from her hands gradually forming into the shape of a horse. The dragon startled Jade with a yawn. Her hands parted; the magic that darted from her hands spurted over the fire, extinguishing it.

"Oh," Dan said. He paused as he was fitting a gear in place, holding the tool with a befuddled expression.

"Sorry!" Jade jumped to her feet and crossed her arms.

"Maybe you should leave that to me," Miria suggested, fumbling to her feet.

"Uh, right." Jade lowered her arms and stepped aside.

Miria crossed her arms and a ball of magic fell onto the logs, and a new fire sprung to life. "Good to know the other realm still answers me with this hand," she said, wincing slightly when she flexed her fingers.

Dan and Jade regarded her with looks of concern as she resumed her place by the fire. Jade inched closer to her.

However, Miria slid back and cleared her throat. “It still feels odd to see a noble not run at the sight of magic,” she said, abruptly changing the subject.

“Well, I have a family history of bucking tradition with unusual interests when they had time to spare,” said Jade, rearranging the book on her lap.

“You make it sound like a hobby,” said Miria, quirking an eyebrow.

“It couldn’t exactly be more than a discreet hobby in Rioda.”

“Now you have to tell us more,” Dan said.

“It’s a long story.”

“Well, we’re not going anywhere tonight,” said Miria. She slid a piece of fish from her skewer and tossed it over her shoulder to the ice dragon, which promptly snapped it up. “Why don’t you regale us with a tale?”

“I was only nine. But I’ll recall as much as I can,” said Jade. She placed her hands atop the book and sifted through her memories.

***

Jade snuck through the castle gardens with an armful of carrots and bandages. She gazed up at the great hall's passageway, where a flustered Shondan marched from the hall. Her husband Carison Sol waited outside the entrance for her and they left together.

"Jade," whispered Kaylen as she snuck up beside her. "Be careful, okay?"

"It's our secret, all right?" said Jade.

"Of course, my first chance with the Royal Guard would go like this," Kaylen grumbled. "It looked so helpless and cute when I found it in the tower. Now I have to go on patrol because of that thing."

"We'll figure something out," said Jade, patting the older girl on the shoulder.

"I'll meet you at the tower later. Don't make any sudden movements around that thing," Kaylen said before scurrying off toward where the guards were gathering.

Jade slinked back into the bushes and crept away as her parents approached.

"Roland's pulling the strings here. She and the other courtiers tried to bribe and persuade me every way they can recently. But they can't do it. The queen won't have it and neither will I." said Shondan. "Jarrod's a new king, left out of the loop and caught up in all the fanfare about the prophecy around him as the chosen king. He just wants to slay dragons. I need to get his attention."

"I know you will. And you've written home." said Carison as he wrapped an arm around her shoulder. Shondan nodded with a heavy sigh.

"I'll think I'll have to go back there soon. I want to show it to Jade too," she said. The side of her mouth curving into a slight smile. "She loves reading books from home. In fact, she loves all kinds of books."

"I know where she gets that from. I'll show her the one I've been studying when she's older," said Carison.

"How is that going by the way?"

"I'm getting there, slowly," he said, rubbing at the back of his head.

"I'm more interested in theory. Darab's web of worlds should be given far more respect than it is."

"Well, Jade's definitely not ready for that."

"The way she's going?" said Shondan, her smile cracking to the side. They both barked with laughter.

Shondan drifted away and cocked her head to the side. "Do you hear that?"

"I guess my heart is still racing," he said, running a hand through his hair. "Oh, what?" Carison moved to stand beside Shondan, whose attention was drawn to the window.

A high-pitched screech pierced the hallways. "I've never heard anything like it before," he said.

"I think I have. Come with me," she said before taking his hand and dragging him deeper into the gardens.

"Where are we going?" Carison asked. Before she could reply, they were greeted by a gaggle of guards who paced forward with the spears at the ready.

"Baron Sol, Lady Shondan. What are you doing out this late?" Captain Sontar asked.

"Just going for a late-night stroll," said Carison as he peered over the man's shoulder. "Ah, Kaylen." He approached the girl with a smile. “I see they finally have you doing more than polishing pods all day.”

“It’s provisional,” said Captain Sontar.

Kaylen gave a quick bow before straightening her posture and wearing an expression of stoic determination befitting of a soldier. “Thank you, Baron. It’s an honor to have this opportunity!”

“Good luck, Kay,” Shondan said as she approached the girl, pressing a hand to her shoulder. “I know you’ll do the Royal Guard proud.”

“Thank you, Ambassador,” said Kaylen, standing tall with her weapon held upright, the ghost of a smile tugging at her lips.

“Well, come now, page; we’re wasting time,” said Captain Sontar.

“Yes sir,” she said.

“You look like you’re about to take on an army.” Carison observed the spears the guards carried with them, tips sizzling with electricity.

"I'm sure you've heard the noise," said the captain. "It's a wonder it hasn't woken the whole damn capital." His words were punctuated by an ear-splitting screech.

"What do you think it is?" Carison asked.

"Not sure, but we're prepared for anything."

"I don't think it's dangerous. It sounds like an injured griffin to me, and a young one at that," said Shondan.

"A griffin?" said the captain. "Never heard of one in these parts before."

"I've only seen them back home, but I read somewhere that they come here in the spring for the berries that only grow in Vansh," Shondan explained.

"Right, we'll keep that in mind," Sontar said, shaking his head, and he waved for the guards to continue. As they marched away, Kaylen peered over her shoulder at the pair. She gestured to the bell tower with a flick of her finger. They nodded. Kaylen offered them a smile before turning her back and leaving with the others.

"Absolute nonsense," said captain when he thought they were out of earshot.

"Yes, sir," murmured Kaylen.

Another cry cut through the air. "We had better hurry," said Shondan. She tugged on Carison's arm, but he didn't move.

"If you want to get to the bell tower, I can get you there right now," he said, extending a hand.

"Oh no," she said. "Are you sure you're ready for that?"

"Hours of work can't be for nothing," said Carison. "Please let me try me try." He extended a hand to his wife which she accepted with a nod. He crossed one arm over the other, brushing one away from him, a blue light flowing from it and engulfing the pair. He closed his eyes and Shondan followed suit.

The pair opened their eyes to find themselves back in Rioda Hall.

"Sol?" Earl Roland turned to the pair, raising an eyebrow. "When did you get back here?"

"Um," said Carison. He continued holding Shondan's hand, turning a deep shade of red. "We forgot to bid you good night." The pair hurriedly bowed and excused themselves from the room.

"Shondan," Roland said to their retreating backs. "Won't you reconsider what we discussed earlier? Once you think about, I'm sure you'll agree it's the best option."

"My answer is still no, Roland," Shondan replied, facing away from her. They closed the door behind them. Shondan shot Carison a grimace. "Maybe we should just walk," she whispered.

"Give me one more chance?" he asked, extending a hand to her once more.

"This better work," she said, slipping her hand into his.

Carison took a breath and crossed his arms, and they materialized in front of the tower.

"You actually pulled it off," Shondan said with quiet amazement.

"Of course," he said with a nervous laugh.

Yet another screech punctuated the air, and even louder than before. The pair dashed inside the tower and up the stairs. In the dark, a frail creature with the head of an eagle and the body of a lion was nestled in a cracked bell, surrounded by carrots. Blood was seeping from its wing. Beside the griffin, Jade tended to the creature, unsuccessfully trying to wrap its injured wing in bandages.

"Jade, what are you doing near that creature? It's dangerous!" Shondan scurried over and crouched down, beckoning the girl to come to her.

"We…I found him," she said as she approached her mother. "He was in a crate in the kitchen stockroom, looking for apples. I snuck him in here where I thought he'd be safe."

"Why didn't you tell us this sooner?" Carison asked, crouching beside Shondan.

"I just didn't want to worry anyone. I thought I could handle it."

Carison's hands were warm on her shoulders. "You can always trust us with the truth and we'll be here to help you, okay?"

Jade nodded. “I’m sorry.”

“What’s important now is getting him out of here, okay?” said Shondan. She shuffled over to the griffin, inspecting its injured wing. The creature lashed out with its claws, and she jumped back in fear and alarm.

“Careful!” Carison ran to her side, kneeling beside her.

“He’s very touchy,” Jade explained.

“I see that.” Shondan looked to her husband. “Could you cast a light?”

“Oh, right.” He rose to his feet. Carison crossed his arms before spreading them, and a blue magic fire hovered over his palm.

The griffin chick calmed somewhat at the magic-induced light. It bowed its head. Shondan took the bandages from Jade and used them to wrap up the creature’s wing.

“I tried to do that. It didn’t work,” Jade admitted.

“I’ve read that you have to close everything else around you and stay in the moment to do magic,” said Shondan. “You did well to get him this far, Jade. This will be our secret, okay?" She hoisted the beast into her arms. "We'd better get him away from here."

"Right," said Carison. He crossed his arm and closed his eyes, concentrating energy into his raised palms.

"Maybe we should go the long way, just to be safe," Shondan suggested.

"Uh, good point," he responded.

As the three descended the stairs, footsteps echoed outside the tower entrance. When they reached the bottom, Shondan crouched behind a stout barrel with Jade and the creature as the door creaked open. Carison froze. He was greeted by King Jarrod, who carried a spear by his side, electricity sizzling at the spikes.

"Sol? What are you doing here?" King Jarrod asked, lowering his spear.

"I was looking for the source of that noise, much like you were, I imagine."

"We don't get many beasts around these parts. I thought I'd better come prepared."

He eyed the crackling spear. "You certainly did that."

"They may be new and in short supply, but I much prefer this to the old sword," he flexed it with a proud smile. "It combines flash and efficiency."

The griffin let out a squawk, prompting Jarrod to rush inside the tower before Carison could react.

The creature leaped from Shondan's arms and bolted from behind the barrel, before crying out in pain and curling into a ball.

"What is that thing?" King Jarrod cried out.

"A griffin," said Shondan. "The poor thing must have been separated from its herd when it was injured. Jade tried to help it."

"I see," King Jarrod said in a slow, measured tone.

"We'd like to take care of the creature while it's recovering if it's not too much trouble," said Carison.

"I'll have to ask you to remove it from here. It's already causing panic and I don't want to disturb the castle any further."

"Of course, Your Highness. We will take it to the nearest forest," said Carison.

"You knew this creature was here, and you said nothing?" Jarrod asked, his gaze falling on Jade.

"I'm sorry," said Jade, shrinking away from the man.

"A fully grown griffin can tear a man to shreds. If its clan heard its cries, people may have very well been in danger."

"She just didn't want to alarm anyone. We'll take the creature away from here now," said Carison.

Jarrod knelt so he was at eye level with Jade. "You must tell me, or a guard when you see something unusual. Understood?"

"Yes, sir," she said.

"Good girl," said Jarrod. He pressed a hand to her shoulder before rising to his feet. King Jarrod paused before turning to leave. "And one more thing: never keep secrets from me again. Understood?" he said, flashing the pair a half-smile. "It's the least you can do for a newly crowned king."

All three nodded. "Yes, Your Highness," they said in unison. The king strolled from the tower.

Carison's gaze fell on Jade. "We'd better take you home, and him to the forest."

***

"Did you ever see the griffin again?" Dan asked.

Jade shook her head.

"I've heard their meat tastes good," said Miria. "He probably took a hunting party into the forest one day and had for dinner."

"Miria!" Dan chided.

"It's a favorite pastime of many kings and lords!" Miria protested. "He seemed a little too eager to use his new toy."

"He's a good king." Jade's tone fell flat. Her eyelids grew heavy as her gaze rested on the southern stars.

"Are you all right?" said Miria.

"It's fine. I'm just tired."

"Jade…" Miria said in a slow, measured tone. "What exactly happened at that meeting in Rioda Hall? What was Roland trying to talk your mother into?"

"And what did the king do about it?" added Dan.

"I'm not sure," said Jade. "I think it was a trade agreement where Marda didn't get the better end of the deal. I shouldn't have mentioned it."

Jade bit her lower lip, her shoulders tensing.

"Maybe we should just get some sleep," Miria suggested.

"No, no it's okay," said Jade. She stared down at her hands, taking a deep breath. "Shortly after that night, King Jarrod made plans to head for Marda. My mother was accompanying him and taking me with her. The king told my mother that he wanted to work with her to negotiate the best deal for both nations. It was around that time, rumors rippled through the court that they had a witch among them. Who, they didn't know, but people began eyeing my mother suspiciously. Some said the rumors of a witch were hearsay, including King Jarrod. Others warned him not to take these whispers lightly since he was soon to travel abroad with my mother. Roland stayed oddly silent until one night when all the courtiers to Rioda Hall for a social function. Everyone was there. Even Kaylen was on duty. I saw her whisper something to a servant and slip a few denarans into his pocket before he began serving all the guests wine. Soon, my mother collapsed to the floor, struggling to breathe. It had been filled with poison."

"Jade…" Dan whispered.

"I was the first at her side…the poison worked so fast." She drew her knees up to her chest and stared into the fire.

Miria shuffled closer to her side. She had no words to offer. Jade unconsciously leaned on her.

"Roland said the servant must have poisoned it as a test, believing the old tale that only a witch could resist poison."

"And they believed her?" said Miria.

"No one would question someone in a position such as hers. The king had the servant executed for the murder of a foreign diplomat. He apologized for the incident each day before he was to leave for Marda, where said he planned to apologize personally to Marda's queen. He said he'd honor his deal with her and drive off the wild dragons threatening the population. Father never practiced magic again after that day, and I didn't either until I left Rioda."

"Your mother would be proud of how far you've come," said Dan.

"Thanks."

"I don't know how you managed being trapped in that nest of vipers," said Miria.

"That's happens when you belong to the world of the royal court," Jade whispered. "My mother wouldn't play along with Roland and paid the price. Just like my father did. He was one of the few people I could trust. That's why I need to reach the Isle."

"I'll get us there," said Miria, a steely resolve lining her voice.

Chapter 16

After they had moved beyond the Vanshian border, the cold gave way to a drier, more arid landscape. They occasionally stopped at one of the tiny islands scattered across the southern region. However, they took fewer stops as they inched closer to Marda, with periods spent in the air that could last for days.

As the night crept upon them, the ice dragon flew closer to the sea with a yawn. Jade leaned forward, tugging at Miria's robes, "We need to stop. The dragon's ready to sleep and so are we."

"It's been an age since we've slept in an actual bed," Dan yelled between yawns.

"Just a little farther, and we'll all rest. I promise. Just a little farther," Miria mumbled, trying to blink away her tiredness. "We're so close."

"We are, thanks to you and our dragon friend," said Jade. "But we need rest. It's what your family back home would want."

Miria sighed. “All right, all right,” she murmured. She instructed the ice dragon to land on the nearest island, and it landed in a village lit with candles.

The lake that surrounded the village had nearly dried up to almost a trickle. A small gathering of water dragons wandered in a confused haze, vainly digging for food, while others slept on the dampened sand, their green scales pale and sickly.

The few people in the town gathered around as Miria instructed the beast to land just outside of town.

“We’ve never had this before,” Dan marveled.

Some pointed to the beast in amazement while others huddled together, speaking in hushed whispers.

“You there,” a woman yelled up at them. “What are doing here in our small village?”

“Riding a dragon,” Miria said with a casual shrug while stifling a yawn.

Laughter rippled through the crowd. “So I see,” the woman said with crossed arms, arching her brow. “Your beast is strangely docile.” The ice dragon stared ahead, breathing deeply and attempting to ignore the unusually large gathering.

"He's well trained, I assure you," said Jade, dismounting the beast. "Good evening. We're travelers seeking accommodation while we rest and recover so we can continue our journey." She stepped toward the ice dragon's head and moved her palm toward its muzzle. The beast pressed its head into her hand.

Words of amazed curiosity rippled through the crowd.

"Well done, Smergo!" Dan shouted.

"We're not calling him that," said Miria.

"And where, may I ask, are you headed?" the woman interrupted.

"Marda," Jade said with a sidelong look to both of her companions. The three of them decided that it would be best if they omitted the final destination of their travels to avoid further mockery or suspicion.

"You are welcome to stay," said the woman. "However, we have little to offer you. This drought has been a terror to our crops." The woman gestured to the barren land behind her.

"We don't often receive this kind of welcome," Jade admitted.

"We are not as fearful of dragons as most. The water dragons here swim beside our boats and help us draw in fish," the woman explained. "Or at least they did."

Dan went ahead to secure rooms for them at a local inn, while Jade and Miria led the dragon away from the village. Now that they were face-to-face, Jade saw a raw, single-minded determination in Miria's eyes, and the coarse familiarity of it made her want to back away in terror. She had seen it every time she looked at her reflection in Vansh's frozen rivers.

"You need to take care of yourself," said Jade. "I can't rescue my father without you."

"I'll get you there. I told you I would," said Miria, grasping at her stone pendant. "I'll do what they couldn't."

***

On a day when the sun shone brighter than the three of them could remember, they drew closer to a large, rounded landmass as barren as the islands.

"It's Marda. It's really Marda! We're finally here!" Jade shouted. "That's probably the sixth time I've mentioned that," she laughed.

"That's the twelfth, but who's counting?" Miria yelled over her shoulder while shooting Jade a playfully exasperated look.

Marda was sparsely populated with only a herd of griffins flying past the rocky mountains and the rare wanderer crossing the vast, empty land. Rusting, broken pod pieces were littered throughout the dunes. The heads of giant metal cats protruded from the sand with a paw and tail occasionally jutting out.

They traveled for long stretches with only the sun and sandy dunes for company. As their journey stretched on, the occasional Tegu dragon skittered along the sand, and herds of griffins soared across the sky.

However, as the ice dragon carried them deeper into Marda, small villages stretched out before them. Aside from patches of green with the odd palm tree gracing the land, they were largely barren and deserted, with only a rare few people roaming the dunes or gathered around a rare watering hole. Beyond the villages was a rundown city encased inside a sand brick wall. On a flat area of land outside the city, no people were present. Yet several camels roamed in an area inside a wooden fence where they drank from a trough. The three of them eyed the spot warily. Miria directed the dragon to land farther along the outskirts of the city. They eased down gradually.

"Is that glass?" said Dan. He pointed to some shiny objects.

The dragon paused before landing on the sand dunes. The area shined with crystalline-shaped pieces of glass, all gathered together.

A low grumbling emitted from somewhere deep below them. The surrounding sand shifted erratically.

"Miria," said Jade, clinging tighter to the reins. "What does that mean?"

"Nothing good," she said and motioned for Jade and Dan to dismount with a flick of her gloved hand.

They fumbled from their saddles and scrambled away.

The beast dug its massive claws into the sand, crouching low as if preparing to pounce, growling at the rapidly shifting sand.

Two sharp, black horns rose from the sand, and long yellow claws began digging their way to the surface. The creature that emerged had a long, slender body and back lined with crimson scales, while its underbelly glistened with a scaly gold. Its large round eyes were wild with rage and it lowered its body, head bent forward and its short, sharp horns protruding upward. The beast lunged forward and charged at the ice dragon locking horns with the beast. The ice dragon pushed it back. However, the desert dragon struck its back with massive claws. The ice dragon cried and stumbled back in pain. Miria marched forward, holding up her stone to the desert beast.

"Over here!" she said, holding up the pendant around her neck as if it were a lifeline. She puffed from heat and exhaustion; her feet planted firmly in the sand. She fixed the beast with an unwavering glare.

"What are you doing?" Dan shouted.

Her small and stout trembling figure was dwarfed by the snarling dragon. The dragon inched closer to Miria, fascinated by the light emanating from the stone. The ice dragon weaved around her and blocked the other dragon's path to the young woman. The beast made a disgruntled sound before turning away and slinking back under the sand.

Jade and Dan rushed toward Miria. Jade gripped her by the shoulders. "Never do that again!" she said before enveloping her in a tight embrace.

Dan followed suit and wrapped his broad arms around the both of them, holding the pair in a tight hug. "I almost lost you to one of those things before. Don't do that to my heart."

"I couldn't let anything happen to our ride, and I had the stone," she said, wrapping an arm around them both.

"You were very brave," said Dan. "And so was Smergo."

"Let it go," Miria said with a snort.

They soon began the task of removing the various straps and belts around the beast and placing the saddles over the branch of a sturdy desert tree.

"At least it's in a protected area where not much sand can get to them," said Dan, hefting his knapsack over his shoulder.

"But a dragon could come by and torch the tree, or someone could take them," Jade said.

"I don't think anyone would want this," said Dan.

"Maybe someone would want to try dragon riding?" Miria suggested.

"You'd need to have a death wish to try that."

She offered her brother a dry look and cocked an eyebrow.

"Okay, I realized the moment I said it! I'm hot and sleep-deprived," he said. "Well, taking himinto town with us would just draw too much attention."

Jade nodded, and the two waited in sandy dunes as Miria tied the ice dragon's reins to the dead tree.

The three ran along the wall, trudging to the entrance. Before they could move any farther, a gust of wind whistled through the air, followed by the sound of flapping. The ice dragon slumped down beside them. The trio's eyes flicked over to the beast.

"What are you doing?" Miria demanded, clutching the stone.

However, before she could raise it, the injured dragon hopped onto the wall and dived inside the city.

"Oh spirits," said Jade. "It's going to cause a panic."

"I'll get control of it." Miria stood back and held up the stone, shooting a blue light across the city. An irritable growl came from the other side of the wall, followed by the wall crumbling as the dragon's thick tail shot through it, making them leap away as pieces of stone flew at them. A gaping hole now stood before them.

"Well, at least we found a way in," Dan muttered.

They crept over to where the ice dragon was curled up under a pile of rubble. It sighed in contentment as it closed its eyelids and drifted to sleep.

“Must be trying to get out of the heat,” said Miria.

Dan took in a breath. “We should still try and get Smergo out of here before—”

“What is this?” a voice yelled from behind them.

They pivoted on their heels and were greeted by several people gaping in a horror at the beast nestled in the rubble. A dark slender man with a wide-brimmed hat and black hair that fell around his shoulders stood at the front of the gathering. He walked with light steps and wore a disapproving frown.

He inspected the three newcomers with raised brows. “Who are you and why did you bring a dragon here?”

“That is hard to explain,” said Miria.

“Try,” said the man.

“Maybe we should leave,” Dan whispered.

“We won’t let anything happen to the people in this town,” said Jade, stepping forward.

The man narrowed his eyes. “Who are you?”

"I'm Jade Sol, the daughter of Shondan, the former Mardan ambassador," she said, stepping back and standing between Miria and Dan. "And these are my two travel companions. They made it possible for me to be here."

"And how did you get all the way out here? Just the three of you?" the man asked. The three shared nervous glances.

He and the others waited for an explanation while clearing their throats and tapping their feet.

"We flew," Dan explained with a gulp, fiddling with his hands and suddenly missing his cap. The gathering shot the young man a perplexed look.

Miria buried her head in her hand. "We came here on this snoozing ice dragon," Miria explained.

"You what?" The group gaped at one another in bewilderment.

"We rode here on the back of the dragon," said Jade. "It's really quite tame. Well, at the moments he's recovering his injuries."

The man nodded in numb confusion. “And what brings you here?”

“We’re headed to the Isle of Dragons,” Miria said curtly, tired of hiding their planned final destination.

Wide-eyed, the man turned to his companions and broke into astounded laughter. “You’re not your average travelers, I’ll give you that much.” The man shook his head with a low chortle.

“We’ve journeyed a long way with that beast, one that doesn’t breathe fire and is under our control. It won’t harm you. I can assure you,” said Miria. The stone glowed brightly underneath her robes.

“We’ve been on the run from the Vanshian authorities. We just need somewhere to stay the night,” Jade explained.

He cocked his head. “Is that so? You can stay now. But if that,” he said, gesturing in the sleeping dragon’s direction, “so much as sneezes, we’ll have to ask you to leave.”

“Agreed,” Jade said with a tired smile.

“Then follow me. I’m Tay Jaden, the town glassmaker.” Tay marched through the town square, signaling for them to follow him with his flame staff.

“We saw pieces of glass along the sand dunes when we ran across a fire dragon,” said Dan.

“One of my main jobs in this town is to give the beasts a shiny treasure to hoard,” Tay explained.

“They’re avid hoarders, right?” said Miria.

“Yes, especially when it comes to glass. We’ve made sure they have plenty, and in return, they stay out of our way.”

“How did you make all of that glass?” said Dan.

“With our most abundant resource: sand. Make it hot enough and you make more than enough glass to satisfy a desert beast.”

“Could I watch you make some?” Dan asked.

Tay chuckled. “Perhaps a little later. For now, let’s go home.”

They entered the town square, and Tay pointed to his workshop before leading them into a white hovel with a thatched roof.

He rapped on the door, and a woman soon opened it and took in the newcomers with a curious stare. She wiped her hands on her apron and tightened her dark bun. “I wasn’t expecting you to bring guests?”

A young girl with curled hair stood beside her mother, a mixture of skepticism and curiosity reflected in her wide eyes.

“Dad’s back already?” asked a boy from inside the home, scuffling to the doorway beside his younger sister.

“How did the patrol go?” asked the woman.

“Unexpectedly. We have three travelers who’ve wandered into our city, and they’ve come all the way from Vansh,” he said.

“Oh? What brings them all the way out here?”

“I’ll explain the rest away from the villagers” prying ears and eyes,” said Tay. “This is my wife, Rose, and our children, Vanda and Matt. Please come inside where we can talk in private." He removed his hat and used it to gesture for the three to follow him inside.

The small sturdy home was made from sand, clay, straw, and water bricks. While Vanshian homes were thickset cottages designed for warmth, the purpose of Mardan homes was to keep out the harsh desert winds. The three stood in the center of the house in awkward silence before Tay waved them to the kitchen table and they gathered around it.

"These three say they traveled all the way from the Kingdom of Vansh on a giant, white dragon," Tay said as his shoulders trembled with remnants of incredulous laughter. "They're on the run from the authorities apparently."

The woman's voice caught in her throat and her gaze fell on the three bedraggled young travelers. "But how? Where is this beast?"

"Snoring among rubble near the crack in the wall," said Tay. "They tell me it doesn't breathe fire and they have it under control. They might even scare a few Vanshian soldiers away."

"Vanshian soldiers?" Jade asked. "They aren't on the battlefield fighting wild dragons?"

The young girl turned to Matt and communicated something to her brother through sign language. "She says the, uh…soldiers are everywhere," he said, side-eying his parents as if conscious of the fact that he should not fully translate the sentence.

"Thank you, Vanda, but there was no need for that kind of language," Rose said while giving the girl a pointed look.

"The soldiers have a base here, probably two the way things are going," said Tay.

"What do you mean?" Dan asked.

"People tend to disappear at times," he explained. "We have some ideas where they might be going, but they don't like us exploring beyond the walls."

Silence settled on the home before Rose cleared her throat. "Could I ask why you're on the run? ?"

"They say they're headed to the Isle of Dragons," Tay explained.

"I'm looking for my family. I think he might be there," Jade explained.

"Rose and Tay exchanged nervous glances.

"Maybe this was a bad idea," said Jade, taking a deep breath. "We shouldn't bother you."

"What do you think Rose?" said Tay.

"I suppose… they need our help," she said. "Come, I'll show you to the spare room." Rose gestured for Matt and Vanda to help as she gathered up spare sheets from a cupboard and led the guests down a narrow hall, with the children trailing behind.

Vanda signed something to her brother while hugging the bedsheet she carried.

"She wants to know if you're dragon tamers," Matt explained.

"She is," said Jade, waving a hand in Miria's direction.

"Dragon tamer, eh?" Miria mused. "I like that."

"Maybe you can start up a business as a professional dragon tamer when we get home!" Dan said with a light chuckle.

"Let's just get to the Isle first," said Miria.

"I apologize, but this is the only area we have for guests. It may be a little snug, but it's all we have."

"It will do fine, thank you, ma'am," said Dan.

"I know you've come a long way, but you'd be better turning back now. Even if you do make it to that Forbidden place, you won't make it back."

"I've heard there are these sky carriages that carry people from Marda to the Isle all the time," said Matt.

"Sky carriages?" said Jade.

"Those are just made up stories that drunken sailors tell to pass the time," said Rose. "At least, that's what we all told ourselves.

After putting her knapsack away and freshening up, Jade shuffled into the kitchen while Rose prepared food. As the woman hummed a vaguely familiar tune, Jade lingered in the doorway a moment. Memories arose from the smells of the spices and herbs. Images of laughter around the dining hall after collecting rare meats and vegetables from the local markets danced through her mind.

"I can get you something if you would like," said Rose, never looking up from her work.

"Sorry! I didn't mean to stare," said Jade. "It's been a long time since I had anything like that. Mother didn't cook often, but she knew a few Mardan dishes."

Rose picked up a carving knife and used it to gesture to several uncut vegetables. "I could always use an extra hand around the kitchen."

Jade nodded before sliding over to the kitchen bench and began chopping vegetables in slow, careful cuts. Rose chopped up the onions with short, sharp motions, dicing the vegetables into perfect thin pieces. Her movements weren't as slow and labored as Gila or Tarin's, with breaks in-between to massage their arthritic joints. The thin, crisp chops were also far more elegant than Dan's long choppy blocks or Elisa's unevenly cut pieces. Rose brushed the vegetables from her chopping board and into the boiling pot and sprinkled a carefully measured amount of herbs and spices along with them. She instructed Jade on each stage of the preparations, taking her through the correct herbs and how long to leave it inside the fire oven.

Matt and Vanda waited at the kitchen table, gazing longingly out at the window. "We want to join the others," Matt complained.

"You will when we're finished here," said Rose.

Vanda signed something to her mother.

"I'm glad you're ready to go now, but you'll just have to wait. You don't want to miss out on the salad I'm preparing?"

They both shook their heads.

"I need you two to make sure all the food is wrapped and ready to go once I'm finished here." Rose promptly turned her attention back to Jade and demonstrated the correct preparation techniques.

"Go where?" Jade asked.

"Town square," Rose explained. "Everyone'll be there for the evening meal since it's the last day of the month. Tay wanted it canceled, but I was having none of it.

The town committee saw it my way, too. We need some kind of normalcy in these crazed times."

"Rose, why are there soldiers here and what do they want? My mother tried to negotiate a trade agreement with Vansh years ago. And Vansh agreed to act as allies in helping prevent wild dragons from overrunning villages."

"Really? Well, that's not how things panned out."

Vanshian soldiers marched by, their eyes inspecting the streets with the keen shrewdness of a vulture observing its prey. One stopped to peer inside the home, his gaze locking on to Jade's. She jumped back, not knowing the man but fearing he recognized her. He turned his gaze from her and continued on.

"Are you all right?" Rose asked.

"I don't know," said Jade, her shoulders tightening.

"You've been on the run too long,'" the woman said, shaking her head. "We'll explain more over dinner."

***

A bonfire blazed in the town square. The fragrance of a dozen herbs filled the air as merchants took down their stalls for the evening. People ate and danced around the fire, trading news and gossip as musicians played a light, convivial tune on flutes and drums. While Jade and Dan engaged in lighthearted chatter with Matt and Vanda, Miria shuffled along beside them, knapsack tucked firmly under her arm with the stone glowing faintly inside it.

"Over there," said Tay. He flicked a hand toward several logs arranged in a circle around the bonfire.

"We saved this one for you, Tay!" A man waved them over with a jovial laugh. The family took their place on the offered seating area, beckoning their guests to join them. Rose unpacked the meals and handed food to them. The smell of the roasted deer marinated in various spices and herbs teemed throughout the town square.

Jade and Dan exchanged bewildered expressions.

"Of course, but please don't be long or you'll miss the evening dances," said Rose. "You can watch us dance." She playfully nudged her husband's arm with a mischievous wink.

"It's been so long. You know I have two left feet," Tay said.

"You'll be fine, glassmaker," shouted a woman in the crowd.

Tay tried to mutter out a response, only to fold his arms and look away in defeat.

The gathering laughed in response to Tay's discomfort.

"Well," said Miria. She gestured for the two of them to follow her.

"We're coming," said Jade.

Dan nodded, standing up with a stretch and wiping the sand from his overalls.

"Make sure to stay where you're not too far from sight. There are soldiers crawling everywhere," Tay cautioned.

"We'll be just over there." Jade gestured to a darkened area by a closed food stall. Tay handed her a lantern, and she thanked him and wandered over to the stall with Miria and Dan.

"Something wrong?" Dan asked.

“Yes, we need to go back to Tay and Rose’s house soon and get our things,” said Miria. “I understand that you’d want to stay here for some time before leaving for the Isle, but it’s in our best interest to leave as soon as possible.”

“Miria,” Dan said. “You know the dragon’s tired and recovering from the fight.”

“They heal fast after a rest. Besides, he’s not hurt that badly. We can’t just wait on it to make a full recovery. The longer we stay, the more danger we’re in. There are Vanshian guards crawling all over these streets. You know this is for the best, don’t you, Jade?”

“The seas are deadly enough without taking an injured dragon with us. You can’t just make the poor creature do whatever you want whenever. He has to guide us back to his home. I can’t help my father if none of us make it there alive.”

“You need to trust me,” said Miria.

“You got us this far, didn’t you?”

“I think its for the best right now,” said Dan. “Besides, Jade should be able to experience a little of her mother's home before we leave. Pushing the beast will only put us in more danger.

"You wouldn't understand," said Miria. "I'm the only one who can carry on our parents work magical creatures."

"No," Dan admitted bitterly, his gaze shifting his gaze away from his sister. "I don't suppose I would understand."

Silence fell.

"Come," said Jade. She pressed a hand to her friend's back. "We'll leave soon."

Jade and Dan made their way back to the bonfire, the music growing louder as people began to dance in circles around the flames. Miria shook her head, a resigned smile tugging at the corners of her mouth. She rejoined the gathering, unaware of the owl that hovered in a circle overhead before disappearing into the night.

Chapter 17

Soldiers watched in silence while standing dangerously close to the townspeople's merrymaking. They eyed anyone who drank too much or caused too much ruckus, their spear tips softly crackling.

Tay and Rose led the dance, their hands pressed together, and circled one another. Tay shot the three an awkward glance as he followed his wife's lead, his movements stiff and awkward. Rose and Vanda giggled at his discomfort.

Jade, Dan, and Miria weaved around the dancers and perched on a log beside Vanda. Jade hummed along to the music while the crowd clapped in concert with the movements of the dancers as they circled around the fire.

When the couple had finished, they gave a hearty laugh and a deep bow.

"Was that 'The Cricket Song'?" Jade asked.

"You know it?" Rose asked.

"Only the lyrics. I never learned the dance that went with it."

Rose darted a slight smile at her husband. "Shall we teach her?"

"I'm not dancing again," Tay huffed. He took a seat while rubbing the stiffness from his back.

"Ah, I tried," Rose said with a shrug.

"I just wish I had my violin," said Dan. "Oh well." He jumped to his feet. "Might as well join in." He accepted the many invitations from boys and girls with a timid smile and a graceful bow.

Jade admired from the sidelines. "I was never much of a dancer," she admitted.

"If this formerly awkward griffin can dance with the elegance of a swan, then you're fully capable of learning at least a few moves," Rose countered while gesturing to her husband.

"A swan you say?" said Tay. "You're too much, but she is a miracle worker to get me to move one foot in front of the other without tripping over."

“All right, come on then,” said Miria, standing upright while brushing sand from her clothes. She extended a hand to Jade.

“What?” An incredulous smile tugged at Jade’s mouth. “But you hate dancing!”

“You need a partner, don’t you? Miria muttered, her cheeks glowing. “We might as well take this chance, right?”

Jade’s eyes widened, then narrowed into a grateful smile. She pressed her hand into Miria’s gloved one. They began to encircle one another to the rhythm of the music.

“This feels a little awkward,” Jade admitted.

“You don’t have to tell me,” Miria said, eyeing the crowd. They were now the only people dancing, and the musicians seemed to play louder than ever before. People shouted words of encouragement or advice as they stepped in awkward motions around one another.

“Don’t pay attention to them, just keep going,” Rose advised. “Remember, it’s not about one leading the other but a tug and pull based on mutual trust.”

Jade eyed the cloaked figures obscured by the night and the surrounding crowd.

"We're staying vigilant," Tay assured, noticing the young woman's discomfort.

She nodded, and the two danced in a way that reminded Jade of a life that only lived in her memories, but their movements were stiff and awkward, not knowing exactly how they should move.

After bumping foreheads more than once and heeding Rose's continued instructions, their steps became more lively and less stilted. The warmth in their eyes and the flickering fire lit up the marketplace with even more joviality than before with the crowd laughing and joining in. The music grew louder and more persistent. When the pair finished and bowed to one another, the crowd broke into loud cheers.

Rose dragged her husband up for another dance. He threw Jade and Miria a weary glare as they rested in the sand with Vanda and Matt laughing and applauding all the while.

Jade removed her notebook and began scribbling figures dancing, creating a step-by-step guide to "The Cricket Song."

"I shouldn't use it for something like this," said Jade.

"Just make sure you leave enough pages for research," said Miria.

"Did you learn that song from your mother?" Tay asked.

Jade nodded.

"Why don't you show her?" Rose suggested. "Just be careful. Things have been unusually quiet tonight."

"Well, I did say I could handle anything that happened." He rubbed his aching joints before fumbling to a standing position.

"Come on then," Tay said as he waved to Jade. I'll just need to fetch my lantern first."

"Where are we going?"

“There’s something I want to show you.” He jerked his head in the direction of the dark, empty alleyways.

“Hey, you lot!” Tay pointed to several people casually talking behind him. “Watch those guards over there while I’m gone, will you? They’ve been oddly quiet tonight.”

The men and women nodded with a brisk, two-fingered salute. Tay collected a staff with fire burning at the tip before motioning for Jade to follow him. She stood and paused, turning to her friends. Dan began telling Matt and Vanda old fables in a deep, rumbling voice that made him sound like Tarin. Miria lounged beside Dan, smiling in tired contentment while she watched him.

“We’ll be here when you come back,” Miria assured her friend with a half-smile.

Jade nodded. She ignored the traces of hesitation in her friend’s tone and followed Tay into the darkened streets.

Chapter 18

Jade and Tay made their way through the empty, winding streets. Finally, they stopped before a high wall. Tay held the staff in front of a sweeping mosaic made up of a collection of vividly colored tiles that depicted a sprawling city with many towering buildings and a herd of dragons flying above it.

Jade traced a finger along the edges of the mosaic. “It’s beautiful,” she said.

“This is from another time,” Tay said with a soft, nostalgic smile. “We had art like this littered through the streets. People used to come all round to see it. This is what many imagine the Isle of Dragons looked like once. We didn’t always call it the Forbidden Isle. There are stories that tell of a time when there was no division between our world and the Realm of Magic.”

“But something broke the trust between our two worlds,” finished Jade, “and the spirits told the seas to keep humans away.”

"You know your lore."

"Do you have any idea where King Jarrod might be?" said Jade as she brushed specks of dirt from the mosaic.

Tay's shoulders jerked upward in a derisive, mirthless laugh. "You have great pods in your nation, don't you?"

"What about them?"

"We are machine makers as well. You probably saw our wild cats littered across the desert. I wish I could show my children the rows of travelers riding through the desert in those beasts. You see this metal?" Tay glided a hand along the mosaic's shining metal frame. "It's made from a rare metal found in these parts. The queen granted your King Jarrod permission to set up mining colonies here, and our resources soon became fewer and fewer."

"That isn't what mother tried to negotiate at all," Jade whispered.

"It wasn't long before he set his sights on a new horizon, one he wanted to oversee himself," he said, clapping a hand down on the mosaic depicting the Isle of Dragons.

"But how?" said Jade.

"Like most things with your king, it's a secret."

"Back home, I think my father might have gotten a little too close to a dangerous truth, so they sent him to the Isle."

"If you make it, you should watch out for the people as much as the beasts. "

"I'm less afraid of dragons than people. At least you know their intentions from the start," Jade murmured.

"You two! What are you doing here?" a voice boomed from the shadows. "You're out after curfew!"

"Curfew has not been enforced," said Tay as he held his lantern up to the shadowy figure.

An old man with drooping eyes and graying hair sauntered forward. The long blue cape of a captain adorned his broad round shoulders, and the golden insignia of the Royal Guard gleamed on his chest. He beat his spear against his palm in a slow rhythm, the tip switched off.

“It is being enforced at this moment,” said the man.

“I don’t believe I’ve seen you before,” said Tay. He raised an arm in front of Jade as the man moved closer.

“You can call me Captain Vale. I’ve had to leave my post for this particular task. I need this girl and her friends to come with me.” The man peered over at Jade, meeting her gaze. “Are we going to do this the easy way or the hard way?”

Jade took tentative steps backward.

“Run,” cried Tay. “Find your friends! I’ll be right behind you!”

The soldier bounded forward with his spear, and Tay blocked his path by thrusting his staff in front of the man.

“If you cooperate, it will make life much easier for your family,” said the soldier.

Tay stepped back, dodging a spark of electricity that shot from the soldier’s spear.

“I’ll get help,” said Jade.

She dashed into the empty streets. Frantic townspeople began to rush past her and toward their homes the farther she ran, locking their doors as soldiers rounded people up. Jade ducked and weaved through the crowd, trying to discern what was happening over the shouts and cries of civilians and knights.

“What’s happening?” Jade shouted at the familiar faces passing her by in the sea of people.

“Leave! Get out of here while you can,” came the faint replies that soon died out in the commotion.

Struggling to keep up with the movements of the rapidly moving factions, she fell to the dirt. Just as she clambered to her feet, a hand clasped hers and pulled her into a dark alleyway.

“Are you that determined to get yourself killed?” said a sharp, familiar voice.

“Kaylen? What are you doing here?”

She grabbed hold of Jade’s wrists while sliding a rope from her side belt and tying the younger woman’s wrists together in a tight knot. “My duty, as best I can now that your antics had me demoted and sent to a desert outpost."

"So that's why Riley was leading the search for me last time. You got demoted."

"I won't be here for long, though. We've been ordered to take your friend's magic stone."

"You leave them out of this. Why do you even need it?" Jade stood in place as she fixed Kaylen with a fierce glare. The fear that gripped her that day on the docks had long disappeared, and a quiet rage simmered in its place.

"It's not my place to ask questions."

"Where's Grant?"

"Still in Rioda."

"Is he safe?"

"You know there are consequences for actions like his."

"What did you do?"

"What did I do?" Kaylen repeated with an indignant scoff, pressing a hand to her chest. "He might be in lock-up, but if it wasn't for me pleading with Roland, he'd be toiling away in a mine on that damned island."

"So now you're telling the truth about what you're doing on the Isle."

"I was sworn to secrecy."

"Grant didn't deserve any of this!"

"He should have stayed out of it," said Kaylen, momentarily averting her gaze. "His family disowned him, embarrassed by his ramblings about that place." There was a slight tremble in her voice.

Jade closed her eyes, and she leaned against the alley wall. "I was wrong about you," she said between gritted teeth.

"I don't take pleasure in any of this, Jade." Kaylen's tone and gaze sharpened.

"That didn't stop you from moving into my family's estate as soon as you could," Jade seethed. "You only ever used me to get ahead."

Kaylen's long, calloused fingers curled into fists. "Think what you like. I earned my position."

"They sent this…monster after us. One of them even attacked the estate they gave to you."

"Who?"

"The court, who do you think?"

Kaylen scoffed, "You'll make up any story to defy them."

"Don't your strings ever get too tight?"

"You never grew up on the streets with only the hope of being something better for company. The Royal Guard took me in when I had nothing. I've learned that if you stay in line you can move closer to the front. Your father lost everything because he strayed too far from it," Kaylen said bitterly.

"All you've learned is how to be a selfish coward!"

Kaylen suddenly dived at Jade, grasping her by the shoulders and dragging her out into the crowd once more. Screams and shouts filled the busy streets louder than before as soldiers led dozens of people away in handcuffs.

People were rounded up and forced to the outskirts of town, receiving a sharp jab with the blunt end of their spears if they protested or moved too slowly. The electrified tips crackled on the other end, a constant reminder of what would happen if they refused to move altogether. Kaylen waved to Captain Vale, who sifted through the crowd while shouting orders.

"Sir, I have the traitor's daughter!" Jade helplessly struggled against her steely grip as she was pulled along the tide of helpless bystanders dragged beyond the town by the droves of soldiers.

A dragon's roar shot across the city, cutting through the crowd's cries of desperation, turning everyone's attention to the skies. The ice dragon glided along like a ghostly specter, lingering just above the crowd. People cried out in shock and panic, and those who had not been apprehended by the soldiers dispersed throughout the city. Others freed themselves from their captors in the confusion or fought back. Miria rode atop the dragon while scanning the crowd.

The soldiers held their weapons by their sides and afraid to use them in case the beast unleashed a plume of fire below. Kaylen stood at the center of the crowd, continuing to help round up citizens. Jade caught sight of Dan sifting through the crowd from the corner of her eye. He gestured in her direction, and people Jade recognized from the town square tackled Kaylen from behind, forcing her to let go.

Dan moved in the direction of the dragon, careening along the streets and waving his arms about frantically. “She’s over here!” he shouted.

When Miria’s eyes locked onto him, she directed the ice dragon toward them. He turned back to Jade and untied the rope around her wrists with quick, nimble movements before tossing it aside. He offered her a sly grin as he pressed a small, rectangular metal object into her hand.

“I’ll see you soon,” whispered Dan.

Before she could respond, Jade felt herself pulled toward the dragon that was hovering nearby. The people dispersed and the beast landed as she was drawn closer toward it. Miria extended her hand and reached down. Jade took it, and she scrambled onto the saddle with the town’s citizens pushing her from behind. Captain Vale turned to the soldiers and ordered them to let the fleeing people go, inclining his head toward the dragon.

"Get off that dragon," he shouted. "This commotion is all because of you and your friends. Hand over that stone so we can end this!"

Miria darted the man a brief glare, then turned her attention to Jade. "Where's Dan?"

Before Jade could answer, the ice dragon began to flap its wings, pushing the people away with the force of the wind that the beast created. One soldier watched the beast's ascent and exchanged nods with Captain Vale before positioning his spear so it aligned with the dragon's chest and launched it into the air. The crackling weapon narrowly missed the ice dragon's chest, and instead, the electric waves coming off the weapon struck the beast's forearm. The dragon let out a roar of pain and continued its rapid ascent into the midnight sky.

The pair held tight to the reins of their saddles. Miria leaned forward. "Come on, come on; we need to turn back," she said in a hushed stammer.

But the beast would not listen. It waved its head about in wild motions. Miria wrapped her arms around the dragon's neck and clung tightly to keep from falling off. The creature's flapping become faster and more frantic. Jade and Miria yelled out to Dan in vain as a soldier handcuffed him, dragging him beyond the city with the others. Their voices faded as the houses below them grew smaller. They held on tight as the beast bucked about wildly, carrying them far from the chaos below.

Chapter 19

The ice dragon hovered over the rubble of an old home and flew in a circle before descending into the ruins. It screeched and shook its head about in frustration. Miria promptly dismounted and examined the dragon for injuries, leaning down to inspect its foreleg, whispering words of rushed assurances to the beast.

"You'll be fine. Rest up."

The dragon hissed in pain and frustration, its nostrils flared with smoke gushing from them. It turned from the young woman with a huff and curled into a ball, wrapping its long silvery tail around its massive body.

Jade fumbled from the saddle and hurried to Miria. "I'm so sorry! This wouldn't have happened if—"

"Just!" Miria snapped, turning on her heel away from Jade. "Just let me think! We'll figure something out." The cracks in her voice betrayed the calm she tried to portray, and she took a breath, her gaze fixed on the slivers of sunlight peering through the cracked stone walls.

“We don’t even know where they took him and the others,” whispered Jade. “Miria—” Her voice was drowned out by a high-pitched electronic squeal.

Miria spun around. “What is that?” she asked.

Jade’s eyes widened, and she stuffed a hand in her pocket. She withdrew the rectangular metal object Dan gave her and held it in her open palm. The electronic sounds grew louder, interwoven with garbled human voices.

“How did you get that?” said Miria as she rushed toward the device.

“Before Dan was taken, he gave this to me. These voices, they sound familiar.”

“Take them…end cell…hurry.” Dan’s The muffled voices yelled in disjointed fragments.

Jade took a step back, the device falling to the sand.

“He must have the other one, and wherever he is…we can hear what is going on where he is,” said Miria as realization dawned on her.

Jade knelt and grasped the device, holding it in her palm. Miria knelt beside her and the pair cocked their heads, listening for any signs of where Dan could be.

"It's like a communicator in a patrol pod," whispered Jade. "Only, he's using voice instead of code."

"I've nearly got it," Dan's muffled voice echoed from the small rectangular object.

"I can hardly hear," said Miria, taking the object from Jade and holding it near her ear. "Dan! Dan, tell us where you are!"

A high-pitched squeal prompted Miria to draw it away from herself. The voices became clearer. "Jade, Miria, sorry…Come…camels…underground."

"Camels," Jade muttered. "They were in an enclosed area with no people nearby—"

"On the surface," interrupted Miria, placing a hand on her chin.

"Dan and the others are trapped in some underground prison," said Jade.

"I don't think he would have come back with us even without the incident back there."

"He…he wants us to come and save everyone."

Miria rubbed her forehead and heaved a long sigh. "Let's just concentrate on getting him back, so we can give him a talking to after, okay?"

"But how are we going to break in?" Jade's gaze turned to the sleeping dragon beside them.

"If the beast was in better condition, we could charge and set the guards aflame," Miria murmured. She rose to her feet and paced while Jade slipped the small contraption back into her robes.

"We need to stay calm and come up with a plan," said Jade, dusting herself off as she stood, her eyes following her companion's movements with quiet unease. "The dragon needs time, and we don't have that. And besides, they'll be expecting us to ride in on a dragon," Jade observed.

Miria abruptly stopped her pacing. She turned to Jade with a large grin, a glint of triumph in her eyes. "*A* dragon. Yes, of course!"

"What are you talking about?"

She ignored Jade and began inching toward the sleeping dragon, sliding a hand under Dan's saddle and snatching up his knapsack. She set it onto the sand and removed some items before sliding it with one arm over her shoulder beside her knapsack. "We'd better get going. We need to make a quick stop at Tay's glass shop."

"Why?" said Jade as she sprinted behind her.

"To find some backup, of course!"

"Glass, of course! But, this…could go very wrong."

"I know," said Miria, sucking in a deep breath.

"Okay, well, let's go!"

Miria crossed her arms and wrapped an arm around Jade's shoulder before they vanished in a swirl of blue light.

***

Jade and Miria appeared before the glass workshop, the sand-swept streets barren.

"Wouldn't it be safer if we magic them to us?"

Miria shook her head. “We haven’t had contact with any of Tay’s pieces of glass. We’ll need to collect them by hand.”

Two soldiers halted in their patrol, gaping at the pair.

“Stop,” one yelled before the pair scrambled toward the young women. Jade and Miria darted into the workshop, shutting the door behind them. Jade fumbled with the locks, pushing tables, chairs, and any other item to block the door. Miria stuffed as many glass items into both her knapsack and Dan’s as she could, breaking some in the process.

As the men thrust their spears through the wooden entrance, splinters of wood splayed across the workshop, and bolts of electricity seared through the furniture.

“Hurry,” Miria hissed between gritted teeth as she leaped away from the assault.

“Going as fast as I can.” Jade rushed to the shelves of glass, stuffing the various sculptures and drinking glasses into her knapsack. “Tay put so much work into these…We need to pay him for these.”

Miria rolled her eyes. “We can make it up to him later,” she said.

The soldiers barged through the door, kicking away the items used to barricade it. Miria slung both knapsacks over her shoulder and made her way to Jade. She crossed her arms and reached out for Jade’s hand, who clasped it tightly. They both disappeared in a beam of blue light and collapsed onto the sand, facing the searing sun and panting heavily.

Jade’s head lolled to the side as she shot Miria a small grimace. “It won’t be enough.”

“It will have to do.” She stood, dusted herself off, and turned to look behind her. There was no sign of the ice dragon. Jade turned and jumped to her feet. She exchanged a panicked glance with Miria. Their gaze shot to the sky and the beast was flying far off in the direction of the Isle. The beast flapped its wings in wild and erratic movements as if fleeing in fear.

“You can’t keep running forever, Jade,” said Kaylen. She and a dozen knights inched toward them, brandishing their spears. Several camels were lined up close by with saddles attached, waiting for their riders to return. An owl shot through the arid air and perched on Kaylen's shoulder. Its pale blue eyes inspected them as its head fell to the side, regarding them with intense curiosity.

"What is that…being doing with you?" said Jade while gaping in confusion.

No one answered her question, and the owl continued to stare, emitting small hoots of curiosity. Miria's gaze was fixed on the retreating dragon. Miria's gaze was fixed on the retreating dragon, and she kicked up the thick coating of sand as she sprinted toward the creature. A beam of blue light shot from her stone and cascaded across the empty skies.

"Come back," Miria cried, straining to raise her tone above a hoarse whisper. Exhaustion and shock had stilled her voice.

Jade could only glower in quiet contempt at Kaylen as their only means of reaching her father faded from their sight.

Chapter 20

"We'll ask you only one more time," said Kaylen. "Your only way of getting out of here is gone and you're too worn out to fight."

Kaylen and another rushed forward. A man clapped handcuffs on Jade's wrists.

Before the other could reach Miria, she shot a beam of blue light from her pendant, blinding everyone except the owl. He swooped towards her, knocking her to her feet before flying away and settling atop a wall. Kaylen marched forward and knelt in front of Miria. She held out a hand, waiting for her to hand over the stone. "You know you can't win."

Miria batted away her hand and stumbled away from her. Before she could cross her arms, Kaylen lunged forward and grasped the pendant snatching it from her neck. She grasped the pendant in one hand, and yanked Miria to her feet with the other. A guard approached Miria from behind and handcuffed her.

“Your friend’s as difficult as you,” said Kaylen as she handed the pendant to a soldier who gave her a barely perceptible nod.

“Well, let’s get moving. The captain will be expecting us,” the soldier said and waved for his cohorts to follow him.

Before they began their trek to the outskirts of the city’s walls, the owl perched on Kaylen’s shoulder tugged at a chestnut lock of hair that had slipped loose from her high ponytail.

“Not now,” Kaylen mumbled. Another soldier chortled behind his hand at her irritation. “Lieutenant?” She threw a questioning look at the man wearing the stone.

He rolled his eyes. “Just make it quick.”

“All right, all right, just give me a moment, Drey!” She removed her knapsack and tossed it behind the wall. The owl spread its wings and glided behind it.

Jade’s gaze fell on one of Dan’s work tools protruding from the sand. The soldier that kept her in place held her shoulders with a viselike grip. Suddenly, Jade collapsed onto the sand, falling on her side.

“What’s the matter with you?” demanded the soldier.

“Sorry, it’s just that the heat is getting to me. So different from home,” said Jade.

“Come on, up you get,” said the soldier. As the man grasped her arm and dragged her up, Jade snatched up the screwdriver and slipped it into her robes.

While they waited for the owl, many groans and human-like sounds came from behind the wall. Jade’s shoulders tensed, and the soldiers shared irritated looks, their eyes fixed on the space behind the wall. Soon, a gangly man in a white, gold, and crimson cloak strode from behind the wall with Kaylen’s knapsack draped over one shoulder. The man approached them with a light skip, offering a slight smile and a two-fingered salute to the soldiers. He had a long bulbous nose and a mess of ebony hair that fell loosely over his round, boyish features. The man tossed the knapsack back to Kaylen, who clasped one of the arms and slipped it back over her shoulders.

His gaze traveled to Jade and Miria; he flashed a pearl-toothed grin at them before waving his arm in a circular motion and bowing his head.

“Jade! I’ve waited so long to meet you in person…so to speak,” Drey said as he waved in the direction of his body.

“Gila made you sound…different,” said Jade, clearing her throat.

“The worst thing I could be is predictable,” he said.

Jade and Miria swapped bewildered looks.

“We’re wasting time!” said Kaylen. They led the pair to their camels where everyone except Drey mounted them.

“Wait,” said the lieutenant, holding up a hand. The soldiers promptly backed away from their steeds. “Check inside their knapsacks.” Two soldiers marched forward and removed them from Jade and Miria, stuffing their hands inside and throwing and sifting shards of glass in their gloved hands.

"Why are these filled with glass?" demanded a soldier as he threw a chipped glass cup over his shoulder.

"We wanted to have some reminders of our time here before moving on," Jade explained.

A flash of amusement briefly traced over Miria's face.

"I suppose you think you're funny?" The soldier shoved Jade to the ground. She collided sideways into the dunes, the grains of sand clinging to her face.

Kaylen flinched. Something snapped in her eyes as if a distant memory came reeling back.

"Sir!" she yelled, turning on her heel and hauling Jade to her feet. She stomped toward the man. "What gives you the right to act like nothing more than a common street thug?"

The lieutenant approached her, eyebrows raised in stern disapproval. "And what gives you the right to speak to one of us like that, *Sergeant*?"

Kaylen averted her gaze and bowed her head. "I apologize, sir. I was out of line."

A desert dragon soared overhead, its wings leaving a gust of wind that fell over the gathering. The soldiers held their weapons high, electricity shooting into the sky.

The lieutenant continued to berate Kaylen while the other soldiers watched on in quiet enjoyment, exchanging amused looks and playful nudges.

"Humans waste so much time over the most trivial things," said Drey, his eyes darting between the pair. "I would have thought you had more important things to do."

The man sighed. "The shapeshifter has a point. Come on, let's get moving. Sergeant, take their belongings. We'll interrogate them when we get back to the prison."

Jade's notebook slipped from her knapsack and fell to the sand. "Wait, please! I need that," she pleaded.

The soldiers ignored her, passing the knapsacks to Kaylen, who stuffed them underneath her camel's the saddle. The soldiers mounted the animals, and they made their slow march beyond the city's walls single-file. Drey stood in place, staring out at the notebook before Kaylen ordered him to move, and he scurried to her side. Jade and

Miria trudged beside Kaylen's camel while the shapeshifter strode alongside them, his steps quick and light.

"You have a strange connection with dragons, don't you, witch?" said a soldier. His eyes were locked onto the skies as dragons soared high above them. He held the camel's reins in one hand and her spear in the other.

"That was my parents," said Miria, her cracked voice lined with bitterness. "I couldn't exactly write another *Life of Dragons* for you."

"*Life of Dragons*?" scoffed another soldier. "Weren't most of the copies burned after the court declared it heretic nonsense?"

"That's because they're liars," she muttered.

"What was that?" the soldier snarled, looking back at her with a sharp glare.

"Nothing," said Miria, raising her voice. "Nothing at all, sir."

"Good," said the soldier, turning his attention back to the front.

"I can see being around her has corrupted you even further Jade," said Kaylen. "You need help."

"I'm not the one who needs help," Jade scoffed, rolling her eyes. The wall's opening loomed before them, and they passed through and into the arid desert. Her gaze flickered to Drey, who'd quickened his pace and softly whistled as he inspected a silver pocket watch, opening up the insides and examining every piece with care. He occasionally asked Kaylen about how a part functioned. She mumbled out several curt responses.

Jade jerked her head toward a pocket inside her robe. Miria caught a glimpse of the screwdriver, and Jade slipped a hand inside and withdrew it. She held it up to the base of their knapsacks and jammed it inside, then pulled at the hole to make it larger, and slivers of glass began streaming onto the sandy dunes.

Drey slipped the watch into the folds of his tunic and slowed his pace to match Jade and Miria's. If he noticed the glass sliding from the back of the knapsack, then he showed no signs of it. Jade stared at the man, regarding him with a mixture of caution and curiosity. He met her gaze and grinned widely.

"I believe you had a question for me earlier, didn't you, Jade?"

"Pardon me?"

"You asked why I was with these fine people here." He waved a hand toward the soldiers. "I've seen the greatest mysteries of the universe, but people are the one puzzle beyond my understanding."

"You want to understand us?" Jade asked. She cocked her head to the side in utter confusion.

"Of course! All of you are so fascinating and full of conflict! Nothing like the other realm! Admittedly, Kaylen's not much fun, but we make good work partners, don't we?"

Kaylen shot a brief glare at Drey before shifting her focus to a host of small dragons that flew overhead.

"Why did you attack us back on the farm? Were you ordered to?" Jade asked.

"Hmm? Oh well, not exactly. I'd heard so much about how unusual you and your friends were, and I just had to see for myself!"

“I’m sorry, what?” said Miria, her head jerking upward.

“I like to listen to the local gossip when I’m town-hopping.”

“When you should be scouting instead,” said Kaylen.

Drey replied with a slight shrug and an easy grin. “I wanted to know if you were as powerful and unique as the rumors said you were. And it turns out they were right! Not many people, let alone ones so young, would try to scare me away! After that, I knew you would do even more interesting things. You passed!”

“That was…a test?” Jade asked, her eyes widening in disbelief.

Miria fumed beside her, making fists around the chains that linked her handcuffs. She rooted her feet in the sand. “You attacked my family for your sick game!”

“Get this situation under control, Sergeant. We’re not far now,” yelled the man at the front of the line.

“Keep walking, witch, or you will regret it,” warned Kaylen.

Miria bowed her head and continued on.

“All this walking is tiresome,” complained Drey. “And don’t you think camels are an unsophisticated form of travel for beings who can make mechanical beasts?”

“I offered you a camel before we left,” said Kaylen, her gaze remaining on the dragons.

“I suppose it would be too cramped and hot inside one of your pod things, but these beasts aren’t much better.”

“We’re almost there,” said Kaylen. A gaping hole in the sand was clearly visible as they drew nearer to the prison.

“Miria…Jade…where are…lost contact,” Dan’s voice blared over the static of the electronic device.

“What is that?” Drey asked.

“What’s happening?” the lieutenant asked.

Jade rooted her feet into the sand, her face panic-stricken. Miria offered her a half-smile, jerking her head behind her. Three desert dragons followed the path of glass with two in the far-off distance, while another bounded toward the party, moving ever closer.

The soldiers dismounted their camels and marched toward the pair while clinging to their weapons as they crackled with electricity. Jade and Miria shrank back, the shards of glass breaking under their boots.

"I think you have something bigger to worry about than us," said Miria.

Kaylen's gaze darted to the torn knapsack, her eyes following the trail. "What is this?"

"I believe it's a trail of glass," observed Drey.

"Why didn't you mention this earlier?" she demanded in a low voice, gripping her spear while locking her eyes onto the shapeshifter, preparing for a fight along with the other soldiers.

"Curiosity?" he offered.

The soldiers halted, and their jaws dropped. A line of desert dragons trailed behind them, following the treasure that had poured from the knapsack. The desert dragon at the front of the line glided toward them just above the dunes before landing, its massive white claws crunching into the class to claim it. The beast snarled at the gathering, its thin white fangs warning them to back away from its new possession.

Miria turned to glare at the lieutenant. “You want to get out of here alive, you need to give me back the stone and set us free!”

“It’s not like you can outrun it,” added Jade.

“Get ready,” said the lieutenant.

“But, sir, we don’t have any chance of killing that creature,” said Kaylen. The desert dragon roared and stomped forward, sand splaying upward each time it pounded a claw into the dunes.

“We can still slow it down long enough to get back to the prison and call on the others.” He released a torrent of electricity at the beast’s chest as it neared closer, hitting its mark. The dragon shrank back, curling in on itself.

“Take the prisoners with you,” the lieutenant ordered Kaylen and another soldier. “And you,” he said, turning to Drey while removing the stone from around his neck and thrusting it into his hands. "You need to take this to Captain Vale and let him know what's coming."

"The man already has a full table," Drey mumbled.

"Something wrong?" the lieutenant demanded.

The shapeshifter shook his head and gave the man a sharp salute. He snatched up the stone and shuffled toward Kaylen, who held Jade's shoulder with an iron grip and guided her forward. The other soldier did the same for Miria.

"I'll go on ahead," he said. While his gaze was locked on Kaylen's, he crossed his wrists and released a tiny sliver of magic with a swift flick of his hands. The magic shot into the keyhole of Jade's handcuffs and they opened with a soft click.

Before Jade could throw Drey a questioning look, his image was soon replaced with that of a barn owl gliding across the arid land with the stone clasped in his talons. Kaylen kept her gaze on the skies while continuing to march toward the prison.

The other soldiers huddled together, preparing to face their enemy once more, their spears lined up, and the combined electricity ready to shoot at the beast again as it collected its senses, unfurling and stretching out to its full height, casting a towering shadow over the soldiers. With smoke flaring from its nostrils and emitting a deep growl, the dragon lowered its body and started bounding toward them.

Jade threw off her handcuffs and brushed Kaylen's arm away, rushing to the scene behind her. She crossed her arms and released a stream of magic. As the soldiers directed a torrent of electricity at the encroaching beast, the lightning blast crashed into a thick wall of magic, with chunks flying away and leaving a gaping hole, smoke flowing from it. Everyone gaped in awe at the sight, the soldiers lowering their weapons. Jade panted from exhaustion and turned to Miria, who the soldier released in the confusion of the moment. The beast collided with the wall and began frantically clawing at it and issuing a piercing screech that echoed through the desert.

"Go," said Jade. She unlocked Miria's handcuffs with a swift motion, and they fell to the sand. Miria gestured to where the stone had once laid on her chest with her fist and shook her head.

"I could—" Jade began before the other woman shook her head in a small, emphatic motion.

"No, you're right," Jade whispered. "You can do this."

Miria closed her eyes and took a breath. She stepped toward the dragon as the magic barrier slowly dissipated into nothingness. The beast stalked forward, still gasping in pain from the electric blast, a large gash across its chest. Miria shuffled closer, creating a tiny ball of magic with her hands, and the creature's gaze fell upon it, regarding the young woman and the light with a mixture of awe and fear. The dragon stepped away, baring its teeth.

"It's okay," she whispered to the snarling beast. "I know they hurt you. But…everything is going to be all right now. I promise."

Miria inched closer, holding the light toward the beast with her good hand. As the blue light touched the creature, the gash along its chest began to heal. While the burn mark was not fully healed, the rawness faded and the beast closed its eyes in apparent relief. The dragon took a step toward Miria and lowered its head, allowing her to run a gloved hand over its head and horns. Her ragged breath began to slow, still holding the ball of light within the desert dragon's sight.

The beast crouched down and dug its massive claws into the sand while lowering its head in a calm, subdued manner. Miria took ginger steps toward its side. The dragon twisted its long neck around to follow the small light still clutched in her other hand. She climbed onto its back, the light from her hands fading away. Jade and the soldiers stood gaping in fear and awe as the dragon strode forward. The camels had bolted off into the desert, desperate to escape the creature. Miria reached down to take Jade's hand, who clasped it tight and scrambled onto the creature's back. Kaylen and the other soldiers dispersed, backing away from them in a desperate attempt to flee the beast as it sprayed fire from its mouth. They dived to the desert floor, narrowly missing its flames.

"What was that you said before, sir?" Miria said, glaring down at the soldiers from atop the dragon. Her shoulders shook with silent laughter as the beast advanced on them.

“Miria,” Jade whispered. “Please, stop. What about Dan? And the stone? We’re running out of time.”

The dragon snapped at the soldiers as they cowered from it.

“This isn’t over,” Miria whispered. She crossed one arm over the other, creating a ball of blue light. She flung it in the direction of the prison’s gaping mouth. The desert dragon’s attention was drawn to the light and bounded toward it.

Chapter 21

Jade clung to Miria's waist, the desert dragon striding ever faster toward their destination. "How did you…," Jade began, searching for the right words.

"I don't know," said Miria in a hoarse voice.

The beast came to a halt beside the prison entrance, the blue flame of magic dissolving nearby. Its nostrils flared, and it began to growl, detecting the scent of people below. Shouts and cries echoed from the underground prison.

"How about you leave this to me?" Jade said as she dismounted. She glared up at Miria, shielding her face from the sun with her hand. "You had best stay here."

"Why do you always have to be like this?" Miria chided. She moved to dismount. However, she paused when Jade rested her hand atop of hers.

"We can't risk losing another dragon," said Jade. "You should stand guard here for Dan and me. I'll see you soon, okay?"

The dragon shifted impatiently. Miria rubbed its neck, whispering soothing words to the beast. Her gaze fell on Jade and she shot her a half-smile. "All right. You have a point."

Jade gazed behind the desert dragon at the soldiers ambling toward them as other desert dragons shuffled along the sand. “We have more company,” said Jade as she backed away.

Miria peered over her shoulder. “Hurry!”

Jade dashed to the prison’s entrance, a thick metal door that stretched high above her. Charges of electricity mingled with frantic shouts echoed on the other side of the door. She closed her eyes and took in a breath, crossing her arms and holding her palms upward.

“Let me in,” Jade whispered before spreading her arms. A stream of pale blue magic shot from her arms and cut along the surface of the door, making a small dent.

Jade panted, shifting from one foot to the other and prepared to strike again. However, the door let out a creak before yawning open to where two guards stood waiting for her, weapons at their side, and prepared to strike. Behind them, a battle stretched along the prison hall, with guards and prisoners exchanging blows with spears, electric sparks darting from both ends of the prison. The cell doors were charred with smoke flowing from them, as if the locks had been burned away with electricity. Among the crowd were Tay, Rose, and Dan. They had gained possession of spears and were fighting off a gaggle of guards parrying and exchanging blows. Dan thrust back one man with a powerful kick and began trading blows with another. Matt and Vanda were huddled behind Rose as she shielded them, fighting off any who approached her children. Those who were too tired and weak to fight crawled under broken tables and inched toward the exit.

Dan caught sight of Jade during the fighting and his eyes widened in fear at the line of soldiers who blocked her path. The soldier he was fighting struck him in the side with his spear, and Dan collapsed to the ground. Jade let out a strangled cry, unable to move past the guards. Tay shot her a sidelong glance before attacking the man, driving him to the ground.

"Put your hands up," barked a man blocking her path, holding his spear level with Jade's chest. The other guards stalked toward her while the prisoners tried to hold them back.

Jade started to raise her hands before crossing her arms and releasing a blue sheet of magic just below the prison's ceiling. Everyone froze in fear and awe. She took a step forward.

"Listen," she said. "My friend is outside with a beast larger and more terrible than you could ever imagine lurking above, and only she can control it. So I suggest you let me turn around with your prisoners this instant." She drew herself up to her full height while taking deep breaths to still the trembling in her hands.

The guards' hold on their weapons slipped as they stared in awe. However, one guard began to chortle, and the rest soon followed.

"Our team scared off your dragon, and we have the source of your power."

The guard stalked forward, while the others turned their attention back to the released prisoners, attempting to round them back into their cells. Massive footsteps began pounding above them, shaking the prison.

"That would be our new friends," said Jade, losing her footing. "We need to get out now! All of you!"

"We'll do no such—" the guard began, before being thrown off-balance.

Kaylen and the other soldiers appeared at the mouth of the prison behind Jade. "This place needs to be evacuated right now," she said. "There are dragons above us! This place is going to fall apart! Get everyone out now!"

Both guards and prisoners frantically dashed to the exit. Dan pushed himself to his feet. He shook off the pain and squinted until his eyes adjusted to his surroundings. His gaze traveled to the trembling ceiling. He frantically pointed toward it. Jade shouted in fear and spread her arms, creating a small domed barrier as a chunk of ceiling crumbled overhead. People jumped away from the sliver of debris that fell from the barrier. Jade's knees trembled, exhausted from calling on so much magic.

Ignoring the cut on her leg, Rose scooped Vanda up in her arms and limped to the entrance with Tay pulling Matt along by the hand.

"Hurry," Rose whispered as she passed Jade.

Dan helped usher people out as he made his way toward Jade. "What's happening?" he asked.

"I'll explain later, but they have the stone," she said between gasping breaths.

"The stone? Where is it?"

Captain Vale weaved through the crowd, pushing his way to the entrance.

"There," said Jade. The blue sheet shattered and the prison's foundations collapsed around them.

Too tired to transport the two of them out, Dan and Jade scrambled away from the prison and dived onto the sandy dunes before it all came crashing down. Prisoners and guards alike were splayed along the sand, many exhausted and injured.

Two desert dragons slashed at the other with claws the size of a grown man and teeth designed to rip through prey with more ease than a carving knife. Miria had fallen off the beast and was shuffling backward on her hand and feet away from the dragons. She clambered away from the fighting and crawled backward toward Dan and Jade. Miria fell on her back to avoid a swipe of the desert dragon's thick tail. She pushed herself up and leaped to her feet, awkwardly bounding through the dunes toward them.

Jade held out a hand to help steady her, which she took. Miria threw Dan a sharp glare before rising to her feet. Do you have it?" Miria said.

"We will soon," Jade said, scanning the crowd. Nearby, Captain Vale was sprawled out on his back, his upper body propped up on his elbows. He was panting from heat and exhaustion. Jade strode toward him with steadfast purpose and a steely gaze.

"Captain Vale," she said. "I'll need you to return the stone now."

"I left it," he mumbled. "It's buried in the rubble."

"Liar!" Jade thundered. "If the king orders something, it's your duty to make sure he receives it at any cost. You wouldn't dare leave behind something that important."

Jade and Miria crossed their arms, preparing to unleash a torrent of magic.

“I suggest you do what they say unless you want to be trampled along with everyone else,” said Dan, gesturing to the dragons behind him.

Captain Vale stuffed his hand inside his uniform and removed the stone, hurling it to the sand. “If you make it alive, he’ll be expecting you, and you’ll lose everything.”

“We already have,” said Jade.

Miria snatched up the stone and fastened it around her neck. It released a blinding light that made all three dragons cower. She turned the stone’s light on the two dragons who had advanced on the other, and they shrank back as the light burned brighter, flying away until only one dragon remained. The light dimmed as she turned her attention to the remaining dragon as it eased onto the desert floor in exhaustion, closing its eyelids.

“I know how you feel,” whispered Miria. “But we’ll need your help again soon.” She rested against the dragon’s side and closed her eyes in relief and exhaustion.

Dan made his way toward Miria. “I’m a little afraid to ask what happened to our Smergo,” he said, eyeing the desert dragon with a mixture of fear and curiosity.

"We're lucky all the guards did was scare him off," said Miria. She turned her back. "He should be nearing the Isle's shores now."

"Miria, I…," Dan muttered, his words petering out.

"Let's just go! Hurry!" Miria shouted to Jade, whose gaze remained fixed on the frightened people stretched across the sand. People made their way back to the township, injured and exhausted, as the soldiers sat in helpless silence, the vicious desert winds whipping their drawn faces. The Jaden family were huddled together on the dunes with Rose pressing a cloth to a cut on her leg.

"I have one more thing to do," Jade whispered. She marched past Kaylen and a human Drey, ignoring them. Drey brushed the dirt from his cloak, pointing at his stained clothing and wearing a pout. Kaylen paid him no heed. She panted in physical and emotional exhaustion, wiping sweat from her brow. Her gaze flicked toward Jade's retreating back, and she held out a hand and opened her mouth to speak. However, her voice caught in her throat, and she lowered her hand.

Drey observed her movements, and his eyes widened upon seeing Jade. He started waving his arms while trotting over to her. "Wait, stop!"

She spun around and threw him a bewildered glare.

“I mean no harm,” he raised his hands in a placating gesture. Jade stood fixed in place and tensed her shoulders. Drey flicked his wrists together before snapping them apart and held out his hands. Her notebook appeared in his palms. “This seemed important to you,” he said, holding it out to her.

“Uh, thank you?” said Jade, tilting her head to the side.

“You’re…welcome?” Drey mimicked her gesture, confusion written on his features.

He returned to Kaylen’s side. She arched a brow, her expression fixed into one of mild curiosity.

He replied with a half-shrug.

Jade scurried back over to her friends and pressed the notebook into Miria’s hands, who regarded it with a bewildered expression. Jade headed over to where the Jaden family was.

“I’m so sorry,” she said, crouching down in front of them.

“We chose to help you,” said Rose as she shakily rose to her feet with Tay supporting her weight and rising along with her.

Kaylen took small, tentative steps toward Jade and the family, who shrank back. Jade stepped in front of the family, rage in her eyes.

"That woman is injured. I can help," said Kaylen as she slipped off one of the arms of her knapsack and began shuffling inside a compartment.

"Don't you think you've done enough?" said Jade, her voice so cold and piercing that the woman took an instinctive step back.

"I was only following orders," said Kaylen.

"I understand. You just always have to be what someone wants," Jade said. "I hope you can live with that." Before Kaylen could respond, Jade crossed her arms and wrapped them around the Jaden family.

They disappeared as pale blue light encircled them and reappeared in front of the family home. Rose limped inside with Tay's help. The children stood frozen in the doorway, shaken with tear-stained faces.

Jade knelt in front of the children and wrapped her arms around them. After parting from the embrace, she untied a satchel of money from around her waist and pressed it into Matt's trembling hands, the weight of it making him stumble.

"I used your glass. And a lot of it," she explained. "This is my last sack of denarans. I won't need it where I'm going, anyway. I want you to take it along with my apologies."

Vanda signed something to Jade.

"She says you should stay away from dragons and strangers when you get to the Isle," said Matt. Jade cracked an awkward, tear-stained smile and tousled the girl's hair. Her gaze fell to Rose and Tay as they made her way to the dining area, where they rummaged through a box full of first aid supplies.

"Jade," Dan's voice scratched out over his device. She removed it from the folds of her robe.

"What is it, Dan?"

"You need to come! Dragon won't wait!"

"I'm coming," said Jade, sliding the device back inside her clothes. "Thank you for everything," she said, turning on her heel to leave.

"Jade, wait," said Rose. "Don't do this. You're up against forces far bigger than yourselves."

"Next time, I'll cook something for you. You have my word as an…ex-noble." She spat out the last word with quiet contempt. Jade crossed her arms and faded into the magic light before reappearing back on the dunes.

Miria and Dan sat atop the dragon's back as it bucked and jerked about wildly.

Dan clung to its back while Miria gripped its horns, urging it not to fly away. When Miria spotted Jade, she extended a gloved hand as the beast spread its wings and hovered above the desert floor. Sprinting to catch up, she clasped Miria's hand and was pulled up with Dan helping her from behind. She fumbled into place between them as the desert dragon rose higher and began soaring through the arid desert air.

"Are they going to be all right?" Dan asked, mounting the dragon.

"I hope so," Jade said softly.

She glanced over her shoulder toward the ground, her eyes locking onto Kaylen, whose expression was fixed into one of dogged stoicism. Jade turned away as the beast propelled them toward the Isle of Dragons.

Chapter 22

Jade woke to the desert dragon's roar. Her head shot up from Miria's shoulder, and she raised a hand to shield her eyes from the sunlight as it stung her eyes.

"Did we make it?" Jade asked groggily.

Miria pointed in front of her. An island lined with lofty trees and mountains that reached the clouds lay ahead of them. The Isle itself almost seemed welcoming from this distance until the wreckage of countless ships sped past them.

Jade leaned against Dan's shoulder while her stomach growled.

"I'd offer you something to eat," he said. "But…" He gestured behind him to where he used to keep his knapsack when they had saddles and an ice dragon.

"Right," said Jade, offering him an apologetic smile. "Sorry. Our knapsacks didn't make it this far, either."

"We can go fishing soon," said Dan. "I hope the Isle doesn't have magic talking fish. I don't think I could eat those." He shuddered at the thought.

"Your device, it's incredible," said Jade. "I hope we can use it on the Isle."

"You think it's incredible? I call it a communicator," said Dan. "I'm just glad we all made it this far."

"Let's just get there first," said Miria. "We could have gotten here sooner with food and our belongings if not for Dan."

"Miria, I'm sorry," said Dan. "People were getting hurt again. So, I put my faith in my work and the two of you."

"It was a huge risk," she whispered.

"*Everything* we do is a huge risk," said Dan. "Most people think this whole journey is suicidal. And look, I'm so sorry about what happened with the dragon. But I had to do something."

Miria said nothing, her gaze fixed on the island. Silence filled the rest of their journey across the sea.

Even though the Isle seemed to be within a short distance, they traveled for hours without coming any closer. The night crept on them and grey clouds rolled over in waves. Clearer skies came briefly as a thick fog drifted in their sight, enveloping them in a mist that blurred their vision.

A light rain descended. It soon passed, the clouds parted, and the dry, arid Mardan air returned. An autumn wind or winter chill zipped through at random intervals. Their journey over the vicious sea drew out for long, painful hours, the waves below them growing larger and wilder with each passing moment. The sea winds that whipped at Jade's hair came to a stop, yet the waters remained as fierce as ever. Small cracks of lightning appeared in quick bursts all around them, making them jump in fear. The lightning stopped as suddenly as it began. The fog slowly cleared, and the clouds parted. The swirling vortex below them began to calm.

"Well, that was interesting," said Miria, holding back a maudlin chuckle. The dragon descended toward a landmass of rock and barnacles with a rounded hole in the middle; the sea raging below it. “Wait. Where are you going?”

“Maybe, maybe this will lead us to the Isle,” Dan shouted.

“Perhaps,” Miria murmured. “I haven’t had time to develop trust with this beast, not like I did with the ice dragon.”

As the dragon dived through the opening, Miria held tight to the dragon’s neck, and Jade clung to Miria’s waist while Dan gripped hers. Once on the other side, the world turned to a deep blue that eclipsed everything. The dragon flew high, its speed steadily increasing.

“What’s happening?” Jade screamed.

“I don’t…I don’t know!” Miria let out a beam of light from the stone, which rapidly dispersed into tiny blue droplets that dissolved into the atmosphere.

Their piercing screams were drowned out as they torpedoed into a vortex of pure light. Everyone’s gaze flitted about the hollow void in silent fear and awe. The dragon drifted through the emptiness until a slither of color gushed into the white atmosphere.

"What was that?" Dan's voice echoed. He pointed to the trail of red that flew across the void. A blue light soon shot into sight, moving toward the red and intertwining with one another in a fluid dance.

The beast began to shoot through the vortex, and more colors shot past, intermingling into vibrant portraits of sunsets, stars, mountains, and oceans. The void created a portrait of the world before their eyes.

Jade's breath caught in her throat. They all screamed in fear and confusion. She blinked, and Miria, Dan, and the dragon all vanished. Jade careened into the void as the colors all swirled together to create a vivid tapestry before her. Thunder, mountains crumbling, waterfalls, and a thousand sights Jade couldn't identify all blended together into one. The rising and falling of the sun, the changing of seasons, and the rise and collapse of civilizations all played out before her in what seemed like a brief flash of time.

Jade closed her eyes and held her head, afraid it would burst from the onslaught of knowledge and sensations bombarding her mind. The sounds gradually faded, and everything slowed until they came to a complete stop.

She began falling, surrounded by nothing but a white void again, plummeting in a realm where time and space had no meaning. All she could do was scream. Her fall came to a sudden halt, and the world grew dark. A single bird sang, waves crashed, and the smell of grass filled the air. Jade clasped a mound of dirt below her. Her eyes snapped open.

A forest with more shades of green than she had ever seen in her life stretched out before her. The forest was sprawling, a gathering of trees whose trunks were far wider and stouter than any pillar in Rioda castle. They surrounded her like ancient and silent guardians. Assorted, brilliantly colored flowers, their gauzy petals drifted through the air, seemingly with a will of their own. The forest glowed with an unnatural aura, with half-heard and seen energies from the earth crackling around her.

A gathering of dragons soared high above the sky. She held up a hand to shield herself from the powerful gust of wind their wings generated.

She pushed herself up. Miria and Dan lay on either side of her in the dirt, unconscious.

Jade shook them both by the shoulders. “Come on, wake up! We made it! We’re here!”

Miria was the first to stir, her eyes fluttering open; she sat up, taking in the land before her, panting heavily. “What-what was that?” She rubbed her forehead, trying to collect her thoughts.

“I don’t know,” said Jade. “But we made it through whatever that was. You did it, Miria!” She bounced on the balls of her feet. However, she immediately regretted that decision and held her head with a groan, still reeling from their journey.

Miria took in her surroundings, eyes wide in amazement, planting her palms into the dirt and feeling the soft vibrations that flowed through the land. A crooked smile of profound joy and awe crossed her features.

“It’s more,” she said, shaking her head. “More…everything than I imagined!”

Dan pushed himself into a sitting position. Once he rubbed the soreness from his head and his eyes readjusted to the world, he gazed in wonderment at the strange and colorful landscape. He stood, helping Miria and Jade to their feet, wrapping an arm around both of them. “You did it, big sister,” he said.

A crooked smile pulled at the edges of her lips. “You both helped…a little,” Miria whispered. The three of them dissolved into soft laughter. But then a sharp growl caught their attention, and they turned their focus to the desert dragon, which glared at the trio before stomping off into the forest.

“Okay, you did most of the work in the end,” said Miria.

“Thanks for your help, Phil,” said Dan.

Miria shot him a bewildered look. “Phil? Are you serious?”

“What? It suits him!”

Jade and Miria swapped amused expressions.

“We should probably start setting up camp and look at finding food,” said Jade as she held her rumbling stomach.

The three explored along the shores, collecting long sticks to use as fishing spears.

Dan sat cross-legged in the sand and removed a boot. “The guards got everything except this,” he said as he snatched a tiny pocketknife from a compartment inside his shoe.

“Always the prepared one,” said Miria while offering Dan a slight smile.

A panicked scream pierced the air farther along the shore, and they made out the outline of a small person pressed up against a ledge.

“That sounds like a child,” said Dan, unbelieving. “In this place?”

“It could be some sort of illusion,” said Miria.

“We should still go look,” said Jade and she began sprinting to the shore with Dan and Miria following along behind her. They halted atop a ledge and observed the beach below them. Along the sand-swept shore was a hollowed-out charcoal tree with twisting branches that ended in small pinchers. A preteen boy was curled up against the ledge, gazing in fear of the tree. A thin branch with thorns jutting from it extended toward the boy.

“Jade, cut it! Cut the branch!” said Dan.

With a quick nod, she crossed her arms and released a stream of magic that cascaded downward and snapped the branch and crumbled to the sand.

"Good thinking," said Jade before clapping her hand against Dan's who let out a slight chuckle.

"Come on, let's go," said Dan.

He and Jade scrambled down to the boy, with Miria following along behind.

The boy's gaze darted to the three strangers approaching him and he backed away.

"Are you all right?" said Dan.

"Where did you come from?" the boy asked. "I haven't seen a person since the mines."

"Now they're sending children to mine here?" said Jade

"People in uniforms stopped at Thane Island on the way to Marda and asked for prisoners. Me and some other kids were in jail for stealing pod parts for our boss. Again."

The boy stood and brushed at his muddied clothes. “I’m Thomas. Where are you from?” Thomas asked.

“From Vansh,” said Jade. “We just arrived here.”

Thomas blinked in confusion. “On purpose?”

Jade crouched down, so she was at eye level with the boy. “I need to ask you something important. When you were working in the mines, did you see a man called Carison Sol?”

The boy shook his head. “Never heard of him,” said Thomas.

Jade nodded and her shoulders fell a little. “Well, this island is huge, after all. How did you get here in the first place?”

“The same way everyone does. On carriages drawn by dragons. No ship can get here.”

Jade swapped knowing looks with Dan and Miria.

“I suppose we’d better get you cleaned up and fed. We were just on a fishing expedition,” she explained.

“You people are weird,” the boy said, gawking in wonder.

“You have no idea, kid,” said Miria. “How did you manage to escape?”

“I snuck out with some other kids when the guards got distracted by the tremors. But I was the only one who made it out.”

“Tremors?” said Jade.

“I don’t understand anything that happens here,” said Thomas.

“Well,” said Dan. “Why don’t we get some food and start exploring together?”

The boy slumped back onto the ground in exhaustion, swapping confused yet relieved expressions.

Chapter 23

The deeper they trekked into the forest, the stranger and more unfamiliar everything became. Flowers and foliage that only grew in certain areas and climates all existed together in a strange union of differing environments. The plants seemed to move with a sense of sentience, their stems growing and intertwining with one another traveling along the forest floor. Thomas strode behind Dan, poking at the flowers with a tentative sense of wonder he hadn't experienced before on the island.

They stopped by clearings filled with unicorns and Pegasi, who seemed unfazed by their presence.

Jade withdrew her notebook and began scribbling away in it, using a makeshift pencil that Dan helped her carve out from the pieces of graphite crystals littered across the beach. Miria listed off all the things she wanted to be written down, and Jade noted each one in detail.

They soon found an uninhabited area near a river to set up camp. Later, they gathered around the fire after finishing preparations for the night and rationing what food they had left.

"Where should we go now?" Jade asked between bites of a meal they threw together with what they had. "This place is so big and strange. I don't even know where to start looking for my father."

Miria gestured toward a small, lone highland peeking above a gathering of pine trees. "Dad used to think hunter serpents had to be real, and they were in these mountains," she said.

"I've been dodging dragons while there was also something called a hunter serpent here?" Thomas said, gaping at Miria.

"They're supposed to be nocturnal, so I could visit its nest during the day," she said. Maybe we could scout out where to go next from atop the mountain?"

"That works. It's the best chance we have to orient ourselves," said Jade.

"What about you?" said Dan, turning to Thomas. "What do you want to do when you leave the island?"

"The only way off here is on a carriage," said Thomas. "We're stuck."

"Hey now, don't you talk like that," said Dan. "We made it here on the back of a dragon. And we'll make it back on one."

"What do you miss most about life back home?" said Jade.

"I don't know," said Thomas. "I guess towns and people. You know, lots of people."

"It's not so bad here, though," said Miria. The look of grim determination that she'd worn since their arrival softened into a brief, reassuring smile. "You'll be okay with us, okay?"

Before he could reply, the flowers recoiled, and the small dragon breeds that sniffed around the campfire scuttled away. A swift tremble soon rippled through the land. Miria was thrown off balance while setting the fire with Dan breaking her fall. She straightened her posture and exchanged a wary scowl with Dan and Jade.

"Miria," Dan said. "What was that just now? Was that…normal?"

"Not sure," Miria admitted. "It's hard to say what's normal here."

"It seems to have gone for now. Those unicorns over there don't seem too worried," said Dan, jerking his thumb over his shoulder at the creatures still grazing nearby. However, after a second, a deeper tremor rippled through the grassy plains, and the unicorns clopped their hooves against the soil in rapid movements and fled to the Isle's shores. Several griffins soon followed. They leaped from tree branches and flew among the trees, weaving around their massive trunks with panicked urgency.

“Because dragons hear at a higher frequency than other creatures,” said Miria by way of explanation.

“If you’re going to tame many dragons, you’re going to need something to attract a lot of dragons,” said Dan.

“Another flute?”

“I can make you another one,” said Dan.

“I started thinking the stone was all that mattered, but you have a point. Hey, uh, thanks,” said Miria.

“No one understands this island, not even the people who brought us here,” said Thomas. “You shouldn’t go exploring.”

Miria brushed her hair back, her gaze traveling far beyond the campsite. “That’s going to change.”

***

When not carving out a new flute, Dan went hunting for deer and rabbits along with Miria. He fashioned himself a spear, while Miria used a ray of magic light to lead animals into traps they configured.

Jade remained with Thomas, teaching him basic uses of magic like creating small balls of light to pass the time.

"This would be easier if I still had Gila's magic book," said Jade. "She's going to be mad at me for losing that."

"I didn't know I could do magic," said Thomas.

"Anyone can," Jade explained. "It's a talent like any other. It takes time, passion and devotion to develop."

A magic fire blazed in Thomas's hands, growing ever larger. When it loomed over him, Jade stepped in to contain it, clapping her hands over it.

"The flame, it was getting hotter," said Thomas.

"Magic responds to your will. If you don't concentrate it somewhere, it goes in its own direction."

Thomas crossed his arms to reignite a small flame in his hand. He stared at it, the corners of his mouth twitching into a slight smile. "If I'd known this before, maybe I could have saved myself and the other kids back home."

"You can't get too caught up in what you couldn't do at the time," said Jade. "I'm still working on that."

"I want to help them, the others on this island."

Jade offered him a half-smile and nodded, swallowing down the uncertainties that still gripped her mind no less than they did before they arrived on the island's shores. "Me too."

"I lost track of how long I was wandering around on my own," said Thomas. "So, I guess what I'm saying is, thanks."

"I'll teach you how to call on objects things, and even transport yourself, later."

Brother and sister marched back to the campsite with a handful of rabbits.

"We have dinner!" Dan announced before sitting around the fire.

They skinned the rabbits before skewering and roasting them over the open flame. After barely touching her food, Miria flipped through the notebook, examining the most recent additions with a discerning eye, and she reached the empty pages.

"Miria, could you help me teach Thomas how to—"

"Not now. We to need leave. Ready?" She snapped the book shut before passing it to Jade.

"I'll keep watch here with Thomas. Just be careful," said Dan.

"If anything goes wrong, we have my knowledge and our magic," said Miria.

Dan shuffled inside his pocket and withdrew a communicator and tossed it to his sister, who fumbled to catch it.

"Brother? You know you can't just appear if we run into trouble."

"You could keep me up to date, right? I don't know how long you'll be gone."

"We'll go up, have a look around, observe the eggs while we're there, and come down as soon as possible," said Miria.

"Could I come too?" Thomas asked. "I can do magic as well."

"You can make dragon puppets who dance," deadpanned Miria.

"The puppets are getting bigger, though," said Thomas. "And scarier."

"I'll make sure the puppet dragons don't get too big while I'm finishing up your flute," said Dan. He waved the near-complete pan flute about, the vines he used as makeshift strings hanging loosely from it.

"Thanks, Dan. We'll be in touch," Miria said as she waggled the communicator about in her fingers.

After saying their goodbyes, the girls descended the path to the mountain.

"You know, you really could write sequel to *Life of Dragons* get back," said Jade. "One the includes all magic creatures."

"What will you once you find your father?" said Miria.

"I already told you. I don't know what will happen."

"Let's keep going." Miria fixed her gaze on a gathering of dragons that flew overhead.

The journey up the mountain was long and winding, and they made the occasional stop for a brief rest before Miria urged Jade on with panting breath. The land began to shake and sent a subtle yet perceptible tremor along the mountain, making the food laid out before them tremble lightly.

"Seems like it's coming from over there," Miria said, pointing to a clearing deep within the Isle surrounded by trees and a wide lake that glistened an unnatural pale blue. A trail of smoke drifted from beside the lake adjacent to a row of tall white tents, the Vanshian flag standing before it. One tall and wide tent stood out among the rest, the one with the king's golden crest stitched above it.

Miria stood and stepped closer to the edge to inspect the area. "Jade, do you see that?"

Jade stood by her side, her gaze sharp and focused as she regarded the scene below them with a slowly festering rage.

Faint shapes and images were reflected in the lake.

"What's that?" Jade's eyes fixed onto the strange shapes, trying to make out what they were. As hard as Jade tried, she could not make out a clear pattern.

"We'll find out later. Come on, we need to keep going." Miria stepped away from the ledge and continued up the mountain.

They walked in silence until reaching the mouth of a squat, dank cave. The pair crept inside, and a large nest made from old grass and leaves sat elevated on a rocky platform looming above them. They shuffled over to it and used the rocky shelf to heave themselves up onto the edge of the nest. Several blue and yellow speckled eggs were nestled beside one another. They watched in silent captivation before Jade remembered her notebook and began busily scribbling notes.

"They're as large as the dragon eggs mother drew in *Life of Dragons*," whispered Miria. She pressed the palm of her ungloved hand against the egg, feeling its warmth. The egg softly trembled underneath her good hand as the cave's floor shook, and the panicked roars of dragons rippled through the skies. Jade's hand began to shake as she sketched out oval shapes. She passed the notebook to Miria, who glanced over the notes before returning them with an approving nod.

“They are slightly smaller than a dragon’s egg,” said Miri, running her fingertips over one. “Could you note that?” The egg trembled under her hand, and soon after, the entire mountain shook. Miria wrapped her around arms the eggs when the shaking increased, preventing them from falling from the nest.

“That was clo—” Jade’s pencil ran off the page and she fell backward.

“Are you okay?”

“I’m fine,” Jade sat up rubbing her back. “But the mother will probably be back soon. We’d better get out of here,” Jade said and stumbled to her feet.

“We need to get an egg first.”

“What? Are you trying to get us killed?”

“I can hold back the beast with the stone. I know I can do it.”

“Miria, what is wrong with you?”

“These creatures are only rumors everywhere else in the world,” said Miria. “I’ll prove they exist one way or another.

There's no need for you to put yourself in danger. You should leave now."

"We're both leaving. Now." Jade snapped the notebook shut and rose to her feet, staring down at Miria with a look that left no room for argument.

A series of pebbles fell to the ground, accompanied by a rumble in the cave's ceiling.

"Did you notice that before?" Jade whispered, pointing to a large opening above the nest.

Miria stood beside Jade, gazing up at the hole, a beast with the head and upper body of a tiger peered down at them and slithered down to its hatchlings, revealing a long, scaled lower body and rattle tail that swung from side to side. The creature hissed, revealing its pearly fangs. The pair backed away from the beast. Miria held up the stone and shined its light up to the creature's eyes. It let out a snarl of frustration, before shaking off the light and stalking toward her. She shrank back, her breath quickened, eyes wide and fearful. Her hand unconsciously brushed over her gloved one, the memory of that night on the farm flashing through her mind. Another tremor rippled through the Isle and Jade stumbled backward. Miria and Jade were shaken, yet they quickly steadied themselves.

“I need a weapon,” Miria whispered while crossing her arms. A line of magic morphed into a dagger in her ungloved palm, her fist closed tightly around it. She snapped her wrist downward, aiming the dagger at the hunter serpent’s heart. It charged at her, its teeth and claws bared. Miria lashed at its upper foreleg. The beast cried out in pain. It slashed at Miria’s leg, narrowly missing. The next tremor threw the hunter serpent off-balance.

“We’re fine, somehow,” said Jade while clutching her head, feeling the beginnings of a headache.

“I almost had the beast,” Miria said, panting wildly and clutching her side.

“It almost had you! What were you thinking? You nearly got us both killed!”

“I told you to leave! I was just doing what I came here to do in the first place; carry on my parent’s work,” said Miria.

“You can’t see anything past yourself!” Jade yelled. “This was only ever about proving you can better than your parents! I should never have trusted you!”

Miria scoffed. ‘I knew it,’ she said. “You always hated that you were forced to rely on us.”

Jade averted her eyes. “You know that’s not true.”

"Miria…," said Dan, stepping toward his sister.

"No, no," she said, waving him off. "I'm right. You never thought you belonged with us!"

Jade darted her a fierce glare. "You only ever used me as an excuse so you could come here."

"Maybe," Miria said softly, shifting her gaze from Jade to the now completed flute lying atop a log. "But you used me to get here. And you never trusted me, not really." She gathered up the instrument by vines tied around it to form a long handle and ran her hands along the varying shaped pipes. "This is better than my old one," she said with a nod of approval. Miria threw it to Jade, who snatched hold of the vine handle. "But you'll need it more than me when you want to get off this place." She approached the edges of the forest, the vast line of trees looming over her.

"Wait, where are you going?" Dan asked, holding out a hand to her.

"Where I belong," said Miria. She closed her eyes and marched into the forest without looking back.

Chapter 24

Night fell and a fragile silence rested on the campsite while they sat around the fire. Jade leaned back on her hands and gazed up at the stars that seem to burn brighter in this part of the world than anywhere else she could remember.

"She'll be back when she's ready," Dan murmured.

A soft tremor shook the land.

Thomas jumped to his feet and swiftly motioned with his hands to create a tiny blue flame in his palm.

"What are you doing?" Jade asked.

"We shouldn't just be sitting here waiting," Thomas said.

"I'm with you," said Dan. "But you know this place doesn't follow the usual rules. We need to make sure we don't get lost."

"But there are people on this island living in big white tents and Miria's going out and doing her own thing while we're stuck here," the boy said, pouting.

Jade closed her eyes before rising to her feet. She picked up a long, thin stick, set the tip ablaze with magic, and a soft blue flame began to burn. “It’s time I got some answers.”

“If you’re going to that campsite, then I’m coming with you,” said Dan, rising to his feet.

“Of course,” said Jade with a slight smile. She snatched up the pan flute and slipped it over her shoulder so she was wearing it like a carry bag.

“You’re just leaving me here with a magic fire?” Thomas protested. “I made it out of a mine by myself!

“No,” Jade said with a sigh. “We can’t afford to split up any more than we have.” She held up the blue flame, and it lit their way as they began their trek through the dark forest, weaving around the massive trunks of the redwoods. Time seemed to lose meaning the deeper they moved through the forest. The island’s time seemed to shift and move, making what should have been a short trip a much longer journey.

They come no closer to the campsite despite night falling away. The gold and orange tendrils of sunlight peeked through the trees. Soon, it was light enough for Jade to put out the flame.

Another tremor tore through the island.

Thomas tripped over a branch and stumbled to the ground.

“Are you all right, Thomas?” Jade asked.

“I’m fine.” His attention shot to a blue light in the distance. “Miria?” He peered through the trees, yet there was no sign of her.

“That could be anything here,” Jade warned.

“Maybe we should check it out?” Thomas suggested.

“Let’s just be careful, okay?” said Dan.

They all crept toward it, their gazes darting about the forest, alert to anything unexpected. The redwoods gathered around a far smaller oak tree like wary protectors. A rectangular stripe of magic in the shape of a thin mirror glowed in the center of the oak. The soft sounds of trickling water flowed from it like a gentle melody. The three of them inched toward it, inspecting the magic glow while keeping their distance. A lush green valley appeared with a creek with clear, crystalline water flowing over moss-covered rocks. Faint cheerful voices rumbled in the distance, mingled with the laughter of children.

"Do you hear that?" Thomas asked in quiet wonderment. "It looks amazing." He held a finger to touch the image.

"Thomas, don't!" Dan cried. But the boy was so entranced that he reached to touch it. He was drawn inside in a blinding burst of light that drove Jade and Dan back, forcing them to cover their eyes. When they opened them, Thomas was gone. The light faded.

Jade screamed and Dan rushed forward and hammered his fist on the oak tree, calling out after the boy. "Wh…what happened? What do we do?"

"I don't know," Jade said, closing her eyes and taking several calming breaths. "We don't even know where he's gone. But we need to remain calm."

"You're right. You're right," he said, letting out a shuddering breath. "We don't have any way of finding him right now, but if we keep going and find Miria, we can figure something out."

Jade nodded, a grimace tugging at her mouth at the mention of Miria. "We just need to keep moving forward and try to get answers. The more we understand, the more we can do later."

They continued on in wary silence, alert for any signs of more unusual happenings. They both jumped when crackling noises blared from inside Dan's pocket. He promptly withdrew the communicator, holding it in his open palm. High pitched static screeched on the other end.

"Miria, she still has the other one," he whispered.

"Where are you?" Jade shouted into the communicator. Half-formed words were cut off by the ringing static. Dan switched the device off and slipped it back inside his pocket.

Jade leaned against a tree. "I don't know where to go."

"Nothing here makes sense," said Dan.

Jade closed her eyes and took in a breath. A faint chorus of hoots mingled together in a haunting song that slowly grew louder and more insistent. Her eyes snapped open. “Did you hear that?”

“It seemed to come from over there,” said Dan, gesturing toward a hilly area north-east of where they stood. “But we better take it slow. We don’t know what it could mean here.”

They slunk through the forest, following the sounds until white tents and a lake began to appear through the gathering of trees in the distance. They froze at the sound of familiar high-pitched cries rippling through the island.

“I know that sound,” whispered Jade. She and Dan shared terrified expressions.

“What should we do?” said Dan.

“We came this far,” Jade said shakily.

As they stepped forward, the outline of a small figure dashed toward them, shooting around the trees in a panic.

Miria stood before them, panting frantically while clutching her chest. "You have to leave now," she said breathlessly.

Dan reeled to her side and placed a hand on her shoulder.

"What are you doing here?" demanded Jade. "I thought you didn't need us."

"The king, he's using one of these to harm people," Miria said, the light of her pendant radiated through her robes and she shoved it in deeper. "Your father's in more danger than you thought if they haven't already sent him there."

"What are you talking about?" Dan asked.

Jade turned to the campsite and moved toward it.

"Wait," Miria whispered, gripping Jade's wrist. "It's too dangerous. I need you to give me the flute now."

Jade yanked her wrist away and threw the pan flute from off her shoulder and into the dirt before sneaking closer to the clearing.

“I’m going with her,” said Dan. He moved to run after her while Miria collected the pan flute, wiping the dirt away.

“I’m going to lure dragons to this place,” whispered Miria. “You need to leave with Jade when they arrive. Dan, I’m sorry.”

“We’ll all leave here together, okay?” Dan said before dashing after Jade. Miria sat cross-legged by a tree with a gaping hollow. She gathered up the flute and played a soundless melody.

***

Jade continued weaving through the trees, glimpsing dozens of tall white tents that were lined up precisely beside one another. They formed a long row which ended in one large tent at the back of the row with the Vanshian flag above it Stern-faced soldiers who held their weapons close to their chests, ready to activate them at any sign of danger, stood in vigilant silence outside the tent’s opening. They remained unmoved by the shrieking cries that pierced the air.

Jade inched closer and stopped in front of a redwood and peered around its massive trunk. Dan crept up and watched on beside her. Beside the lake was a cage with pale, screeching dragons like the one that had attacked them back on the farm. Dan and Jade shared looks of horror. The writhing creatures stood in sharp contrast to the still waters of the crystalline lake that lay nearby, reflecting an image as vivid and awash with color as any an artist could bring to life on a canvas. The image of a grand, sandstone castle, its tall and sturdy embattled parapets and broad high towers shined through the ripples of the lake. Before the lake stood a rune stone with intricate carvings with the sun, moon, and stars.

"Look!" Dan whispered, pointing to the hole in the surface of the rune with a glowing blue stone embedded in one side.

A man with short-cropped blond hair and eyes fixed into a stern glare stood before the rune. He wore a gold crown and a silver cloak that rest heavily on his broad shoulders.

Behind him, several guards dragged a group of people tied to one another by a rope around their wrists.

They were all lined up behind the rune, their wrists chafing against the ropes as they tried in vain to free themselves. They were all thin and their eyes deep and sunken, as if they had not slept in days. Jade recognized among the captives the man from the Mechanic's crew who had come to rescue her.

King Jarrod opened a book and raised it to his face with one hand while placing his other hand atop the stone. He read from the book in a murmur so low that no one could hear the words he uttered. The water twisted and swirled, forming a vortex that caused a tremor to tear through the Isle. The people tied together behind the rune were drawn into the vortex, stepping forward seemingly against their will. They fell inside, screams of terror accompanying their fall. Steam rose from the vortex before it closed, yet the trembling continued. The land became dry in its wake. King Jarrod took a breath before opening the book and chanting incoherently once more.

The lake turned red, and thunder began to crack. From the depths of the water, several creatures burst forth with pale, slithering bodies covered in mucus, and with throbbing veins, and wide, empty white eyes. They screeched in a deafeningly high-pitched tone. Everyone except for King Jarrod covered their ears, the cries reverberating throughout the forest floor, causing the ground to shake once again.

Several soldiers advanced on them with their spears and rounded up all except one in cages. The remaining creature was corralled into a harness and attached to a tall, long blue and white carriage with a coachman perched atop it. Once the dragon-like beast was secured to the carriage, it flapped its wings and took off into the sky, pulling the carriage across the grey sky like a specter of death.

Dan and Jade shared horror-struck looks. “Miria was right,” Dan said in a chocked whisper.

Jade’s gaze lingered on the scene a moment longer, unable to look away. King Jarrod snapped the book shut and turned to the men behind him with a solemn bow. As he marched from the rune, two soldiers called out to him. They marched forward while dragging a handcuffed Miria behind them. There were no signs of the stone’s glow around her.

"Sorry to interrupt, sir, but we found this girl while patrolling the woods," said a soldier. "She was playing this." He passed King Jarrod the pan flute.

"Interesting," he said, inspecting the instrument before handing it back to the man. "What's your name? There's something very familiar about you."

She said nothing, her eyes downcast.

"Answer him," demanded a guard.

"I'm Miria," she mumbled.

"Well, Miria," said King Jarrod. "Is there anyone else here with you?"

"No, it's just me," she replied flatly.

"I see," Jarrod said in a slow, contemplative manner. "Well, I'd like to ask you a few questions, if you don't mind."

"What are we going to do now?" Dan whispered to Jade, curling his fingers into fists against the redwood.

"I…I don't know," Jade admitted. "Doesn't seem like she has the stone."

"She must have hidden it," said Dan.

They backed away from the redwood and snuck through the forest, trying to find the spot where they had last seen Miria.

"There," hissed Dan, pointing to a blue light burning behind a tree.

Jade froze, her eyes flickering around the forest floor. "Do you hear that?" she said.

Two soldiers marched from behind the trees, brandishing their crackling spears. "I knew she couldn't be out here on her own," said a soldier. "You can tell the king why you're here."

Jade's pulse rang frantically in her ears. She moved to cross her arms but was too exhausted from their long trek through the forest to fight, and she lowered them.

The guards attached handcuffs to her and Dan's wrists and marched them down the hill, passing the tree where the soldiers commanded them to halt. A thin blue sheet of magic fell over the tree's hollow.

"The girl put this up when she saw us approaching," said a soldier, knocking on the barrier. "Why?"

Dan and Jade regarded the man with a perplexed look.

"I'm sorry, sir, but we have no idea," said Jade.

"If you won't tell us, you can tell the king," said the man. The soldiers led the pair down into the campsite and toward King Jarrod, who was talking to Miria.

"I thought you came alone?" King Jarrod questioned Miria. She gave a slight shrug in reply.

"Bring them here," King Jarrod commanded.

They led the pair forward and pushed them beside Miria, who shot them a questioning look, jerking her head in the direction of the tree hollow. Jade and Dan kept their heads down, not wanting to meet her gaze.

"You," said King Jarrod, approaching Jade. His eyes held an almost eerie calmness. "You are Sol's daughter, aren't you?"

Jade shrank back under his gaze.

"I haven't seen you since you were a small child! How did you get here?"

"Are you the one who sent that thing after my home, after us?" Jade whispered.

King Jarrod offered her a genuinely regretful look. "I am sorry, truly," he said. "Unfortunately, I had no choice, but I'm glad to see you are all right. If you're here, then you must be the girl with the stone?" He quirked an eyebrow at Miria.

"I…I lost it…before we arrived on the Isle."

"Then what did you put in the tree hollow back there?" King Jarrod asked.

"Nothing. There was a dragon's nest there. I thought your men would disturb it."

King Jarrod lifted a hand to his chin. "Where did you lose it?"

"Over the Isle's seas, Your Highness" said Miria.

"I see." He closed his eyes as his shoulders fell. "Well, since you're here, you must stay with me. You'll have to show my men where you've been staying, so my soldiers can collect your things and bring them back here."

"Why do you need the stone, Your Highness?" said Jade.

"You see this." He gestured to the lake. "This is the gateway to the Realm of Magic. I can summon beings from it with this stone. I have mined the caverns for metal, but it is nothing compared to this!" He waved to the castle in the water. "We only barely made it here when we sailed in my ship." He rubbed his forehead as if trying to chase away a persistent headache. He offered Miria a tired smile. "And your mother is the only reason I made it here."

"What?" Miria whispered. Both she and Dan froze.

"Oh yes, she made all this possible," said King Jarrod. "She even showed me this entry point between worlds! A place where you can do anything. For the right price."

"Price?" Jade asked.

"There's always a price, and these were criminals," King Jarrod said with a dismissive wave. "To expand an empire, you need people to help build it. They're redeeming themselves by helping to extend our reach in the world. Families will be able to live here! We'll set up colonies. But this water…it's like fire to touch." He removed a cloth from his pocket and let it fall into the waters where it burst into flames. "I could hardly believe it when Roland sent me that report about soldiers running into a girl with a blue stone! Combining the two will allow us to finally open the gateway. We were able to achieve so much in Marda, and we're achieving great things here as well. I just need your help."

Miria and Dan's gaze fell to the rune, their eyes distant and unfocused as the king's words swirled in their minds.

"It was you, wasn't it?" Jade whispered. "Of course it was."

"I'm afraid I don't know what you're talking about," said Jarrod.

"Roland tried to manipulate my mother into being your puppet for your agenda. But when she wouldn't follow along, you had my poison my mother. Didn't you?"

The king's hand tremored for the briefest moment before steadying it. His expression remained impassive.

The soldiers cried out in anger. "Did you just accuse your king of murder?" A man stepped forward with an ignited spear.

King Jarrod held up a placating hand. "It's all right. She's just confused. You know I would never want any harm to come to your mother. She was a trusted. I enacted swift justice on the murderer. You know that. It seems your time on the run has had an effect on your mind. But I can help you." He motioned for the soldier to remove her restraints; he moved to her side and unlocked them. Her handcuffs fell to the ground with a soft clank. "I know where your father is," he said.

Jade raised her head and meet his gaze for the first time.

"I can reunite you with him, and I'll even pardon him."

"Your Majesty?"

"I think we both know what's really in that hollow," he said, motioning his head toward the forest.

“It’s clear your new friends have coerced you into using magic, but if you swear to give it up and fetch the stone for me, all will be well.” He reached out a hand to Jade, offering her a smile that held a quiet reassurance. “You can have your old life back.” He reached out his hand a little farther. “You know that you never belonged with them.”

She took a step back and crossed her arms. A burst of blue magic flowed from her hands and a blue shield fell over her, Miria, and Dan.

“What are you doing?” King Jarrod growled. His eyes blazed with confusion and rage. Soldiers uselessly hacked at the barrier with their spears.

“I’m sorry, Your Highness, but I can’t help you,” said Jade.

He thrust his fist against the barrier. “Have you forgotten who you are?”

“No,” Jade said, holding herself up to her full height, “I’m a witch.”

Miria and Dan watched on in quiet awe. The soldiers continued beating at the barrier, electricity ricocheting from it and spiraling through the sky.

"Call in the shapeshifter!"

"Yes, sir," said a soldier before rushing off to complete his task.

The soldiers began to chip away at the barrier. Jade removed Dan and Miria's handcuffs with a flick of her wrist, and the three edged closer together.

"Jade," said Miria, a slight tremor in her voice, "I—"

A roar cracked through the sky and the outline of a dragon weaving around redwoods careened toward them. The sound of grinding gears and the yells of people soon followed.

"It worked! It actually worked!" Miria whispered.

The soldiers' assault on the barrier stopped abruptly as they turned their attention to the forest.

Wolflike pods and several men and women marched from the forest followed by a dauntingly sized ashen dragon soaring toward them with a cloaked rider sitting astride it. They barreled through the canopy and descended on the campsite.

The dragon circled above the barrier, and its rider signaled for it to land. King Jarrod took several steps back, just stopping short of the lake.

Jade, Dan, and Miria gazed up at the skies, the barrier dissipating as the dragon glided in beside them with surprising grace. It snapped at the king and the soldiers gathered around him with spears at the ready.

"No need," said Jarrod, waving them down. "She wouldn't dare let anything happen with them here."

The dragon rider shushed the beast before dismounting, and the smaller figure stood between them and King Jarrod.

"I'm afraid you've caught me at a bad time, Marlow," he muttered.

The rider removed the cloak's hood and turned to them, revealing a woman with long smoky brown hair streaked with white, and wide dark eyes that carried a strong will and deep sadness.

Miria took a step back. Her blood ran cold. Dan's fingers shook by his side and he took in a ragged breath.

"Mother?" Miria whispered.

Chapter 25

"Daniel? Miria?" said the woman in a hushed whisper, as if she were questioning if what she saw before her was an illusion. She took a tentative step forward.

"How?" Dan questioned, shuffling away from Jade and Miria, and approaching his mother. "What happened to you? What have you been doing all this time?"

"I've survived," she said, her tone clipped and bitter. "I can't believe it's you. You're actually here." Her voice slightly trembled. She and Dan rushed forward to embrace one another in a tight hold, both crying in joy and confusion. She parted from the embrace. "How did you even get here?"

"Miria," muttered Dan, awkwardly waving his hand toward his sister. "She helped us get here on a dragon. Two actually."

The woman choked back an astonished chuckle, wiping at her tear-stained face. She held out an arm to Miria, who remained frozen in place beside Jade.

"Why?" Miria whispered.

"What are you talking about?"

“He said you helped him to do all this. Is this true?”

“Miria, you don’t understand,” she said. She took small, careful steps toward her daughter, who shrank back.

“Where’s Father?” Miria asked, never looking at her mother.

“He didn’t make it here. I barely did,” she whispered.

“As much as I enjoy seeing this unexpected reunion, can I ask what prompted this sudden visit?” King Jarrod asked in a clipped tone.

“Our dragons were losing their minds over something and wanted to head in your direction. I didn’t want to risk them all over what could have been a false alarm. But some friends insisted on tagging along.” Marlow shot him a roguish wink.

A roar pierced the air, and a giant winged lioness flew out of the trees, soaring through the campsite, and driving the soldiers back.

Suddenly, a fight broke out between the two factions, with clashing spears and the wolf-shaped pods racing to where King Jarrod stood. Several people stood atop the heads of mechanical snakes that wound around the trees, while archers prepared their bows, releasing a flurry of arrows to the battlefield below.

"The dragon," King Jarrod ordered the soldiers. "Stop it! Don't let them escape!" He removed his spear from behind his back and ignited it. As the dragon dived at them open-jawed, he tried to thrust his spear into the beast's mouth, but it clamped onto its center and tossed it aside and raised its long neck up so it was looming over the men. Marlow stood by the beast, petting its side. Jarrod beckoned for a soldier to hand him their spear, which they promptly relinquished. He circled the crackling spear around the beast's most vulnerable spots, preparing to take aim as the soldiers withdrew in fear.

Marlow marched in front of the dragon and stood in front it, raising her head, her eyes boring into Jarrod's with unnerving intensity.

While the soldiers continued retreating, Jarrod glared up at her wide-eyed. His spear trembled as his grip faltered.

"You," he whispered, shaking his head as pure contempt shone in his eyes. "You've always seen me as weak! You think I won't do it?" Before he could advance on her, she pulled her spear from the inside of her cloak and staved off his attack, the spears locking against one another.

"Get on," she said out of the side of her mouth, throwing her children a sidelong glance. "My dragon will take you to safety. Follow the wolves back."

"We still don't know where Thomas is," Dan whispered.

"What are you talking about?" Miria asked.

"We can find your friend later, go," Marlow hissed. "I'll catch up."

"Soldiers, help the others," Jarrod ordered his men as he fixed his stance, spear at the ready.

The soldiers scuttled away to prepare for battle.

"You were always one for drama," he said.

"And you've always liked the sound of your own voice a little too much. You must have talked the poor kids' ears off!"

Jarrod and Marlow circled one another in an old familiar dance before clashing spears, parrying, and narrowly dodging blows from the electric spikes.

Dan pressed on his sister's back, pushing her forward. "Come on," he whispered. They both clambered onto the dragon's back. "Come on." Dan turned to Jade who stayed fixed in place.

"Go, I can get the stone back." Jade raised her palms and crossed her arms and disappeared in a spiral of light.

"Jade, wait," said Miria who thrust out a hand to Jade as a blue light engulfed her and carried her away.

When Jade appeared before the tree hollow, Drey stood beside it, dipping his hand inside the barrier. Before she could collect her thoughts, she rushed forward and tackled him to the ground. He fell to his back with a groan.

"Is that any way to treat someone who helped you?"

"Why are you doing this? Why are you with the king?" Jade growled as she thrust her palms against his shoulders, pinning him to the ground.

"You ask many questions. An admirable quality." He pushed Jade off him with ease and scrambled to his feet, striding in front of the hollow and waiting for her to stand. "If you want it, you need to go through me first."

Jade pushed herself up, taking in deep breaths. She fixed him with a relentless glare before releasing a stream of magic that spread across the earth and shot toward Drey. He swept a foot along the encroaching blue light and it petered out into nothingness.

"Trying to put me off balance," he observed with a thin smile. "Good, but you will need to do more tha—"

Jade cut him off with another burst of magic that Drey blocked with his arm, brushing it aside with a flick of his wrist.

He shook his head, his shoulders trembling with soft laughter. "You are good."

He released a stream of magic that Jade promptly side-stepped. Before she could move into position for another attack, a blue thread of magic sprung up from the soil and curled around her wrists like a thick rope, dragging her to her knees.

"Magic might look like it disappears after we used it, but it's always there," explained Drey as he paced back and forth as though he were giving a lecture to a student. "It just goes back into the atmosphere." He halted in his tracks, his gaze flitting about warily. "As fun as this has been, good things never last, do they, grandpa?" he asked the man who materialized behind him in a spiral of light.

A bald man with distant eyes stared down at Drey with faint disapproval. "Don't call me that," he said in a soft monotone before releasing a spiral of magic that hurled Drey backward into a tree. The shapeshifter gasped in shock and pain from the blow. The man shot thin lines of magic that snapped around Drey like thin ropes before diving toward the tree hollow and snatching up the stone. He flicked his fingers toward Jade and released her from the magic. When she fumbled to her feet, he tossed the stone to her and she caught it in her palm.

"Come on! We have to go," he said.

“Who are you?” Jade asked, leaning against a tree and panting from exhaustion.

“I can take you to our base,” he said, marching behind a redwood.

She watched his movements in dazed curiosity. The bald man morphed into that of a winged lion. The beast trotted toward her and crouched to the ground, waiting for her to climb on his back. Jade tentatively climbed onto the lion’s back, slipping her legs in front of his wings and clinging tightly to his mane. After stretching out his wings, the lion rose into the sky and weaved through the forest. Jade peered over her shoulder at Drey and from the corner of her eye caught sight of a spiral of magic. It zipped toward them, cutting the lion’s lower thigh. A pained roar rippled through the forest as the lion slipped somewhat, making Jade tighten her grip on his mane. He wildly flapped his wings as they descended faster and faster beyond the battlefield.

“No, slow, slow down,” Jade yelled as the giant lion careened into the dense shrubbery with a low, guttural groan. Soldiers turned their heads from the battle and soon bounded toward the pair. Jade took a shaky breath and rooted her feet into the ground and crossed her arms. As they charged toward her, their spears ignited with electricity, a blue translucent barrier in the shape of a small round shield shot from her hands. The blow pushed her back, smoke flowing from the center of the shield.

When another man shot a stream of electricity at the lion, Jade deflected again, pushing her up against the lion. Jade clapped her hands together and focused the magic light into a blade that shot forward and cut through the metal and the spear's tip and slid to the ground with a thud. The others gaped in horror yet continued forward. Jade created another, smaller shield as she panted in exhaustion. Her gaze darted up to the sky where Miria and Dan circled around the battlefield from atop the earth dragon.

"Look, there she is!" Dan pointed down at where Jade shot a beam of magic into the air.

Miria pulled on the beast's reins and it descended to the battlefield, driving the soldiers back as the creature swooped down in front of Jade and the lioness. Dan waved his hands about wildly at a mechanical wolf, gesturing to the fallen lion, and it hurried to their location. They clambered from the dragon before it touched the earth and rushed to Jade's side.

"Are you hurt?" Miria asked, grabbing her by the shoulders.

Jade removed the stone from around her neck and pushed it into Miria's hands. "Where's your mother?"

"Still busy," said Dan, peering over his shoulder to where Marlow and Jarrod were fighting.

Marlow's eyes flicked over to where her child stood and she shoved Jarrod with a kick, making him fall onto his back. She struck him with a piercing glare while electricity crackled threateningly over him. "We'll finish this later." She dipped her hand into the folds of her robes and withdrew a handful of glowing blue powder and crossed her arms before tossing it to the ground, the smoke engulfing her. Jarrod coughed and fumbled to his feet as she disappeared in a puff of smoke. She reappeared in front of a now human man who sat up in the shrubbery, holding his injured leg.

"Ugh, the little blighter got me! We need to hurry and get the kids out of here," he panted.

"Ah, Amos! You always have to make things awkward!" said Marlow, tossing her cloak onto the man, who wrapped it around his shoulders. She mounted her dragon, waiting as the wolf pod jogged behind them and squatted low, its side hatch cracking open, and Jade scrambled inside with the passengers helping her and Amos onboard.

Marlow gestured for her children to climb onto the dragon. Miria and Dan shared a look and nodded in silent agreement.

“We’re going with her,” said Miria. They both climbed aboard the wolf as Marlow directed the beast into the air with a sigh.

The inside of the wolf was wide and lined with railing, designed to fit about a dozen people inside.

“Hold on tight,” the driver said, turning to his passengers before starting the engines.

With a massive leap, the machine raced through the forest as soldiers began to advance. Its pace grew faster, leaving the Vanshian soldiers behind them. Jade squinted as she stood behind the pilot. A tree in the distance appeared to glow for a brief flash. She blinked in confusion, peering at the tree to check if she had imagined it.

A sudden crack echoed through the forest as a tree began to crash down as they approached it. The pilot thrust the controls, making the machine jump away, jerking the passengers backward. A thick branch thwacked down onto the wolf’s foreleg. The pilot swore under his breath while he lowered the mechanical creature to the ground.

“They’ll be here soon enough,” the pilot whispered, peering over his shoulder at the encroaching soldiers.

"Where is your base?" Dan asked, leaning on the railing and trying to regain his footing.

"Not far," yelled the pilot.

"Maybe we can help," said Jade, exchanging a knowing glance with Dan.

"What are you planning on doing?" Amos asked, holding a bloodied cloth to his leg.

The sound of the soldiers' cries grew louder.

"We need to cut off the machine's leg and create a temporary replacement with magic," Jade explained.

The pilot spun in his seat and glared at her. "Well, it's not ideal, but it's the best we have right now. But don't try it alone."

He gestured at the people behind him, jerking his head in the direction of the hatch. It snapped open with the flick of a switch and Jade, Miria, and three other passengers filed outside, the soldiers growing closer.

Lifting her arms, Jade clapped them together and released a long stream of light from her palms, and soon, Miria and the others joined her, creating a sharp beam of light that cut through the wolf's leg, releasing it. They refocused the magic around the beast's leg, willing it into the shape of a glowing blue limb. Everyone scrambled back inside as soldiers began to charge at the wolf pod, aiming their spears at it. The hatch snapped shut, and the pod rocked with an electric surge running through it as the pilot raised it up and pushed the lever back. The mechanical beast bounded from the soldiers and weaved through the trees deeper into the forest.

"Well," the pilot whispered. Awed whispers spread around the pod, and passengers huddled close to the three young travelers, clapping hands on their shoulders and thanking them.

"That was some quick thinking," Amos mumbled between gritted teeth, while others knelt beside him, trying to stem the bleeding.

"Just an old trick we picked up," said Jade. "Thanks for saving me, by the way.

"I was just trying to stop Drey from getting that stone."

"What do you know about this?" Miria asked, holding up the stone.

"Too much," he muttered. "That is complicated and a story that will have to wait for another time," he said.

A giant cave stood before them, a translucent magic barrier stretched across its mouth. Several people waved their arms about and released a spurt of magic that brought it down.

The metal wolf slipped inside it and trudged along the damp surface in awkward, jerky movements, its metal footsteps echoing through the wide, empty cave with only the sounds of dripping water accompanying them. The passengers made the second barrier fall away before they finally reached the other side. The wolf stepped into a grove lined with tall mossy rocks. Marlow's dragon flew a short distance in front of them and appeared to perch in midair, but the clank of metal underneath its claws indicated it was resting atop a metal wall.

The mechanical wolf leaped over the rocks, dipping forward slightly as the pilot pulled at the controls to force the machine into an upright position, its new appendage struggling to remain in a solid form.

"Don't worry. We're here now," assured the pilot.

Another barrier bubbled along a carbuncled hollow sycamore tree with branches that protruded and twisted about like multiple probing limbs.

When the final barrier melted away, the metal wolf trotted through the hollow and on the other side. A sprawling village stretched out before them, and the people gathered around to see the pod. It trod forward before grinding to a halt.

"All right, take it down," said the pilot.

Jade and the others stretched out her hands, and slowly, gently let the ball of magic slip until it dissipated into the atmosphere, and the wolf eased onto the ground with a soft clunk.

The side hatch snapped open, and they descended the ramp.

"Come on, you three, you'll be staying here now," said the pilot as he rose from his seat with a stretch. He motioned for them to follow before rushing to help Amos descend the ramp along with the others.

A grand hall sat at the heart of the village; a symbol of a winged lion and a dragon standing opposite one another was emblazoned above the door. Thick, towering redwoods encased it with stout rounded treehouses built around them, and long spiral ladders snaked around the trunks. Families dashed onto the balconies to watch the earth dragon soaring back into the village, the riders waving at people as they passed. Marlow brought it to a gradual descent. She led the dragons to a large domed building with water and animal carcasses, freeing them from their reins and allowing them to eat and rest inside the enclosed area.

A crowd of people promptly abandoned their activities and rushed to Amos's side, asking about his injury.

"There's no need to worry about me," he grumbled. "After some rest and five cups of tea, I'll be fine,' he said.

"You still have some worries, old friend," said Marlow, weaving through the crowd and reaching out a hand. "I'll be needing my cloak back!"

His gaze dropped, and his eyes widened at the sudden realization that he was wearing nothing but her cloak.

"Ah, excuse me a moment!" Amos crossed his arms, and a simple white tunic and slacks appeared on him. He slid the cloak off his shoulders and held it out to her, clearing his throat.

"Now, if you'll excuse me, I need to get to the infirmary." Several people led Amos down a path to a large building where men and women rushed to help him inside.

A group gathered around the mechanical wolf, assessing the damage. A woman stalked toward the front of the crowd and inspected the leg with a carefully trained eye.

"Those miners can't wait too long for us to have running machines when we leave for the Northern region," said the pilot, observing the damage from a distance.

"Don't worry, Salen. We're going double time today," the woman said as she scooped her dark hair up into a high bun.

"Well, Sal, there you have it," said Marlow as she approached them. "And just so you know, I've never seen Korla do anything less than double time," Marlow teased from behind the woman. "It's not good for your health."

"Running off on your dragon when it gets skittish isn't, either," said Korla. "What happened back there, anyway?" Her sideways gaze fell on the three standing nearby, and her eyes widened in shock. "Marlow, are they who I think they are?" She stood a head shorter than Marlow with short-cropped hair and a dark complexion. She spoke with a soft voice that held a quiet strength.

"My children, and—" Marlow darted a questioning look at Jade.

"Jade," said Miria, her voice cold. "We wouldn't be here without her."

"You didn't come here in a carriage?" Korla asked.

"We came here on a dragon, by ourselves," Dan explained.

"They really are your children," she said with an astonished grin.

Several people hurried over to the newcomers and began bombarding them with a series of questions about who they were and how they arrived on the Isle.

"Yes, well, could you please give us a moment alone?" Marlow said in a low, cutting voice.

The crowd promptly backed away while making hurried apologies. Korla headed to her workshop, ordering her team to drag the broken wolf away, leaving Marlow with her children. Jade stepped aside to allow them space.

"I have so many questions. I don't where to start," said Dan.

"I know how you feel," Marlow said with a hushed chuckle.

"Why did you leave?" Miria asked in a clipped tone.

"We'd planned to bring you all here someday. I can't tell you how sorry I am. For everything. What happened to your hand?" She stepped forward and reached out to her daughter's gloved hand.

Miria's hand shot away from her mother's. "Why did you help him?"

"That was years ago. I had no choice. I did what I had to, to protect you all after your father die—"

"Protect us?" Miria interrupted, holding up her gloved hand and laughing bitterly. "You failed at that a long time ago." She stalked away.

"Miria! Wait!" Dan called after her. He followed his sister before throwing a hesitant glance at his mother. Jade followed them both, ignoring Marlow's pleading expression. Miria marched off, watching Korla's team haul away the mechanical wolf with ropes and pullies. She paused and turned to face Dan and Jade, rubbing her arm while averting her gaze.

Miria breathed deeply and took a tentative step forward, her eyes locking onto Jade's. "Jade, I'm sorry. I really am. I messed up."

Jade closed her eyes and sat in the grass, slipping her hand into her side belt and removing the notebook, flipping through its pages. "We've been through a lot together," Jade said without inflection.

"I understand. Forgiveness isn't something you can just give, like it's nothing," said Miria. Her gaze fell on her mother's retreating back. "So, be mad at me for as long as you need."

Jade's lips quirked into a half-smile. She tucked the notebook back into her side belt.

"I might have ruined my last chance of finding my father," Jade said with a heavy sigh. "If that's even still possible."

“That man,” said Miria, “he said he used to be a miner and they’re working to free others. They might have information on your father.”

“All we can do now is figure out a way forward,” said Dan.

Miria offered a hand to Jade. “On our own terms,” she said, a coy smile tugging at her lips. Jade took the offered hand as she rose to her feet.

“Salen!” Dan yelled, rushing over to him before he and his crew moved back to their workshop. “What can you tell us about the mines?”

“Mines?” Salen repeated as Jade and Miria, and Dan surrounded him. “Amos is heading that operation. This rescue mission happened in the middle of an attack plan.”

“Attack plan?” Jade asked.

“These people saved me, but there are still many more out there, too many.”

“We found a boy from one,” Dan explained. “And he’s gone missing. We think he could be in a valley somewhere with people.”

“We’ll send out a search party for the boy as soon as we can,” Salen promised. “Marlow will get her riders on it.”

"I'm also searching for my family," said Jade. "I think—want to think—he's alive, Baron Sol."

"Rumors of nobility coming to the Isle spread fast, and not as one of the king's guests, either. It's not every day that happens."

"Do you know if he's still alive?"

"If anything happened it would spread across here like dragon fire. I'd say he's still with us."

Jade's shoulders sagged, and she closed her eyes, relief washing over her.

"We'll get him back for you soon. You can rest now."

"I want to go with you. You saw what happened back there. I can help," said Jade, her tone unwavering.

"I appreciate the enthusiasm, but you'll be safe here," said Salen.

"The three of us made it all the way on our own," said Miria. "We're not exactly great at playing it safe."

He sighed. "You'll have to talk to Amos, but first, we need to get you three cleaned up. You're a mess."

They suddenly became aware of how their dirt-covered clothes clung to them.

“We would really appreciate that,” Jade said with a nervous laugh.

“Come on, there’s a spare lodge that you can stay in for now,” said Salen, leading them through the crowd and to a stout home nestled in the center of a redwood. He motioned for them to follow him up the spiral staircase.

When they reached the treehouse, Salen turned to them with a tired smile. “Not much about this island makes sense, but we’ve made a home here.”

Jade lingered atop a step, taking in the village’s vastness. People busily roamed about, crafting machines and practicing magic, while performers put on a dragon puppet show for children.

“I never let myself think about it too much before,” said Jade. “But I think I’m starting to.”

“Think about what?” Miria asked.

“What my future could look like. I mean, really look like.”

***

Jade, Miria, and Dan marched into the infirmary at the crack of dawn, and a nurse directed them to Amos’s room. He sat upright in his bed, gazing out at the window, his shoulders slumped, and his hands folded in his lap. For a spirit from another realm, he seemed so frail and humanlike.

"Hello," said Jade as she softly rapped on the door.

Amos jerked his head toward the doorway, sitting up a little straighter. "I guess it's that other time I talked about. Well, come on in then," he said with a heavy sigh.

"We would like to come with you when you go to the mines in the northern region. I hope I might get closer to finding my family, and I believe I could help."

"You proved yourself capable. Just don't try to take on a shapeshifter again."

"Why is Drey helping the king?"

"Drey is a child who thinks of this realm as his personal play area. He cares for nothing but his own enjoyment. No shapeshifter has lived here as long as me, and I'm the oldest of all of them. The others don't think too much of me, and the feeling is mutual," Amos said, his shoulders heaving up with a cackling laugh.

Miria took a seat beside him and held up her stone. "I need you to tell me more about this."

His smile fell. He took a breath and regarded her with a somber expression. “That, along with the other stone, are the key to opening the gate between our two worlds. It allowed humans to cross into the realm. When the peace between the two realms was broken, so was the stone, and no human could enter the realm again. But one day, a foolish chaos spirit stole one half of the stone, and searched for a human to gift to, hoping they could reunite the two pieces and unite the two realms once more.”

“You gave my parents this stone, didn’t you?”

“I can only apologize for trusting too much in people. It’s only thrown both worlds out of balance and everything is in chaos. The other spirits were right about humans. There are exceptions,” he waved a hand outside the infirmary window at the village. “But that’s all they are.”

Miria averted her gaze, having nothing to say.

“Maybe someone could unite them one day,” said Jade.

“The only thing we can do now is keep that thing away from that man who calls himself a king and his cronies,” said Amos.

“We had a boy with us who seemed to enter a magic gateway through a tree,” said Dan. “What was that?”

"There are gateways to different parts of the Isle that open up now and then. It's all part of the interference going on. Salen tells me the riders are searching for him."

"About that," said Miria. "I want to stay and help search for Thomas."

Dan gawked at her. "Stay here? With Mother?"

"I'll live," she said with a small shrug. "Besides, I want to help, and maybe I could learn something from these people."

"I'm coming along to help free the miners," said Dan. "Maybe we'll even find the Mechanic and the others."

Jade offered Miria a broad smile. "Good luck, witch."

"You too, witch," she said, returning the smile. "I'll be waiting for you to return."

"I know."

"This place will be a lot for you kids to adapt to," Amos warned.

"I think we'll be all right," said Jade, wandering over to the window. Miria and Dan joined her. Jade pressed a hand to Miria's shoulder as the three gazed out far beyond the village.

Epilogue

The mechanical wolves leaped away from the campsite. Injured men stumbled back to their quarters.

King Jarrod panted, wiping the sweat from his brow as he took in the scene with a scowl, his fists shaking in rage.

Drey strolled through the wreckage with a curious gaze. “Well, they certainly did a number on this place.”

“You’re not here for your powers of observation, shapeshifter,” said King Jarrod. He turned to the man, regarding him with cold resolve. “I need that stone. Find them at any cost and report to me immediately. Understood?”

“I’ve told you I work best with my partner,” said Drey. “You know she still wants her captaincy reinstated.”

“You seem to forget your place,” said King Jarrod, both his gaze and tone sharpened.

Drey shivered from the chilled winds and rubbed his hands together; the friction creating tiny shreds of magic that sprayed around him.

"It is always in the skies, doing as I'm told." Drey offered the king a thin smile. "And Kaylen and I came the closest to delivering what you want than anyone. Would it be wise to ignore that?"

King Jarrod arched a brow. "Start your search now. The sergeant will arrive along with the next shipment of convicts. Don't let me down."

Drey gave a sweeping bow before transforming into a barn owl, which then split into a dozen others. They shot into the skies and began their search, flying over a web of thick vines where a sleeping Carison Sol was trapped inside.

Printed in Great Britain
by Amazon